The huge shape stripped back its hood, and as Conan started in spite of himself, hundred-fold laughter rolled from the mirrors. An ape's head glared at him from atop the scarlet robes, as black as pitch and with gleaming white fangs made for the ripping of flesh. Its eyes held malevolent ebon fire. A tiger's claws tipped its thick, hairy fingers. Slowly it shredded the robes, revealing a massive, ebon-haired body and heavy, bowed legs. No sound came from it, not even that of breathing.

The Adventures of Conan,
published by Tor Books

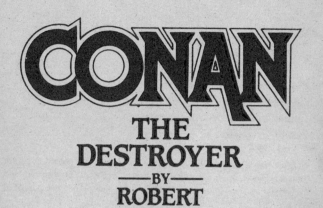

CONAN
THE DESTROYER
—BY—
ROBERT JORDAN

A TOM DOHERTY ASSOCIATES BOOK
NEW YORK

This is a work of fiction. All the characters and events portrayed in this book are fictitious, and any resemblance to real people or events is purely coincidental.

CONAN THE DESTROYER

Copyright © 1984 by Conan Properties, Inc.

A Tor Book
Published by Tom Doherty Associates, Inc.
175 Fifth Avenue
New York, N.Y. 10010

Tor ® is a registered trademark of Tom Doherty Associates, Inc.

ISBN: 0-812-53136-1

First edition: July 1984

Printed in the United States of America

0 9 8 7 6 5 4 3

To Shere Khan

for his invaluable aid

with the script

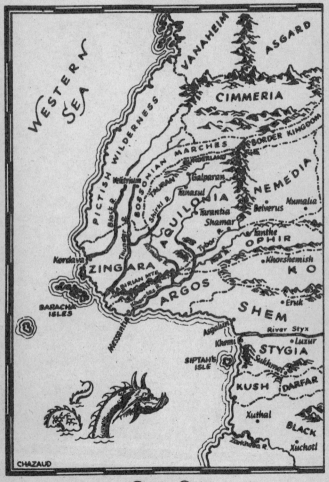

WESTERN SEA

VANAHEIM

ASGARD

CIMMERIA

PICTISH WILDERNESS

BOSSONIAN MARCHES

BORDERLAND

BORDER KINGDOM

Velitrium

Galparan

Tanasul

AQUILONIA

NEMEDIA

Belverus

Numalia

Tarantia

Shamar

Xanthe

OPHIR

Black R.

Thunder R.

Shirki R.

Tybor

Khorshemish

KO

Korvela

ZINGARA

RABIRIAN MTS.

Khorotas R.

ARGOS

Eruk

Messantia R.

SHEM

BARACHA ISLES

Asgalun

River Styx

Khemi

Luxur

STYGIA

SIPTAH'S ISLE

Sukhmet

KUSH

DARFAR

Xuthal

BLACK

Zarkheba R.

Xuchotl

CHAZAUD

Tundras

Haloga

HYPERBOREA

Deserts

BRYTHUNIA

Steppes

KEZANKIANMTS.

HYRKANIA

CORINTHIA

ZAMORA

TURAN

Sultanapur

KHITAI →

KARPASH MTS.

Shadizar

Arenjun

VILAYET
SEA

TH

KHAURAN

Isle of
Iron Statues

KHORAJA

Akif

Aghrapur

Deserts

Samara

Zaporoska R.

Zamboula

Khawarizm

Sagara

Kapur

Kuthchemes

Ptelon

Ilbars R.

KESHAN

Kassali

Kahla

PUNT

VENDHYA →

KINGDOMS

ZEMBABWEI

IRANISTAN

I

The bloody sun baked the Zamoran plain, and baked, too, the procession that made its way across those rocky flats and rolling hills. The riders were armored in ebon breastplates and nasaled helms. Sable was the chain-mail that covered their arms, and sable the greaves that rose from booted feet to dark-breeched knees. No accoutrement of theirs but was the hue of deepest night. Their horses, too, were sheathed in black iron, chanfons and crinets covering heads and necks, peytrals protecting their chests. A long, curved sword hung at each warriors' hip, and spike-headed maces swung at every high-pommeled saddle, but the hands that should have grasped lances held instead wooden clubs and long staves. Nets did they carry, as well, thick woven and weighted, stout enough to hold tigers.

Last in the procession was a high-wheeled cart, drawn by two horses, and on it was bound a large cage of iron bars as thick as a man's wrist. The cart's driver worked his long whip ceaselessly across the backs of his team, for despite the heat of the sun and the weight of their armor the column kept a rapid pace, and it would be more than his life was worth did he delay it a moment in reaching its goal.

He who led the column was a head taller than any other man there, and broader of shoulder by more than a handspan. He was marked as a warrior of note, a man of position, by the intricate gold chasing of his gleaming sable breastplate, elaborate arabesques surrounding a leaping lion. It was a symbol he had chosen many years before, and many said he fought with the ferocity of that beast. Thin, age-whitened scars, one across the bridge of his broad nose and another running from the corner of his left eye to the point of his chin, proclaimed him no newcomer to the profession of arms. Now those scars were all but hidden under dust that clung to the sweat pouring from his face.

"Useless," he muttered beneath his breath. "No Erlik-accursed use at all."

"There is always a use in what I do, Bombatta."

The big man stiffened as one of the riders, masked in soft black leather as well as helmeted, galloped up beside him. He had not thought his voice would carry further than his own ears.

"I see no need," he began, but the other cut

him off with a voice distorted by the mask, yet carrying the note of command.

"What must be done, must be done as it is written in the Scrolls of Skelos. Exactly as it is written, Bombatta."

"As you command," he replied grudgingly, "so do I obey."

"Of course, Bombatta. But I hear a question unspoken. Speak it." The tall warrior hesitated. "Speak it, Bombatta. I command you."

"What we now seek," Bombatta said slowly, "or rather where to seek . . . surely *that* cannot be in the scrolls."

The black-masked rider's laugh was muffled behind the dark leather. Bombatta colored at the mocking tone.

"Ah, Bombatta. Think you my powers limited to knowledge of the Scrolls? Do you think I know only what is written there?"

"No." His reply was as curt as he dared make it.

"Then obey me, Bombatta. Obey, and trust that we will find what we seek."

"As you command, so do I obey."

The huge warrior dug his heels into the flanks of his mount, careless of the men behind who must keep up. More speed, he knew, would be taken as a show of obedience, a sign of trust in the commands he had been given. Let the others mutter angrily in their sweat. He kicked his horse again, ignoring the lather that was beginning to fleck the animal's neck. His doubts were unshaken, but he had been too long in climbing to his present post to lose it now, not if he had to gallop men and horses alike to their deaths.

The plains of Zamora oft saw unusual sights, so often that few were any longer truly considered unusual by those who witnessed them. Madness, bandits and holy vows had at different times produced a man in the robes of a noble who scattered gold coins to the sands, a column of naked men mounted backwards on their horses, and a procession of maidens, wearing naught but blue paint from forehead to toes, who danced and chanted their way through blistering heat. And any who sought to link event with cause would find surprises.

There had been many others, some stranger still, yet few had seemed odder than the two men laboring far from any city or village, beneath the blazing sun in a hollow at the foot of a rock-strewn hill. Their hobbled horses cropped sparse, tough grass nearby.

The first man was a tall, heavily-muscled youth. Massive arms straining, he lifted a thick, flat slab of rock, as long as a man was tall, atop four gray boulders he had rolled together. To level the slab he pushed fist-sized stones beneath it. About his neck, on a rawhide thong, hung an amulet of gold in the shape of a dragon.

The sapphire-eyed young man seemed more a warrior than a builder. A broadsword of ancient pattern hung at his belt, and both its hilt and that of his dagger showed the wear of frequent use. His face, a square-cut black mane held back from it by a leather cord, showed only a lack of years to the casual observer. Those who looked deeply, however, could see several ordinary lifetimes' experience written there, lifetimes of blood and steel.

The sky-eyed youth's companion was his antithesis both physically and in occupation. Short, wiry and black-eyed, with greasy black hair tied behind his neck to fall below his shoulders, the second man stood to his thighs in a narrow pit, laboring to deepen it with a broken-handled shovel. Two bulging leather sacks sat on the ground beside the hole. Continually the wiry fellow dashed sweat from his eyes and cursed work of a sort he was unused to, but whenever his gaze fell on those sacks he set to again with a will.

Finally, though, he tossed the broken shovel aside. "It's deep enough, eh, Conan?"

The muscular youth did not hear. He frowned at the thing he had built. It was an altar, something with which he had little experience. But in the harsh mountain wastes of his native Cimmeria he had learned that debts must be repaid, whatever the cost, whatever the difficulty.

"Conan, is it deep enough?"

The Cimmerian eyed his companion grimly. "If you hadn't opened your mouth at the wrong time, Malak, we'd not have to bury the gems. Amphrates wouldn't know who stole his jewels, the City Guard wouldn't know who stole the jewels, and we could be sitting in Abuletes' tavern drinking wine, with dancing girls on our knees, instead of sweating out on the plains. Dig it deeper.''

"I did not mean to shout your name," Malak grumbled. He fumbled open one of the leather bags and scooped out a handful of sapphires and rubies, emeralds and opals. Green glittered in his eyes as he poured the polished stones back again, a sparkling stream of blue and crimson and green and gold. With a regretful sigh he tugged the drawstring tight. "I just didn't think he would have so much. I was surprised. I did not do it apurpose.''

"Dig, Malak," Conan said, looking now at the altar rather than the other man.

The Cimmerian closed his big hand around the golden amulet. Valeria had given it to him, and it seemed to him he felt her near him when he touched it. Valeria, lover, warrior and thief all in one bundle of lithe golden-haired beauty. Then she died, ripping the joy from his life. He had seen her die. But as well he had seen her return, come again to fight at his side, to save his life. Debts must be repaid.

Malak had taken up the broken-handled shovel again, but instead of digging he eyed the altar. "I did not think you believed in the gods, Cimmerian. I've never seen you pray.''

"The god of my land is Crom," Conan replied, "the Dark Lord of the Mound. At birth he gives a man life and will, and never another gift. He will not pay heed to votive offerings, nor listen to prayers or pleadings. What a man does with the gifts Crom has given him are his own affair.''

"But the altar?'' Malak prompted when he fell silent.

"This is a different land, with different gods. They are not my gods, but Valeria believed.'' Frowning, Conan released the dragon amulet. "Mayhap her gods listen, as the priests claim they do. Perhaps I can do something to help her fate with them.''

"Who knows what will sway gods,'' Malak said, shrugging. The wiry thief lifted himself from the hole and sat crosslegged beside the leather sacks. "Even the priests do not agree, so how can you—'' The clatter of galloping hooves from beyond the hill cut off his words.

With a yelp Malak snatched for the leather sacks. In an instant he had thrust several of the gems into his mouth—his face contorted painfully as he swallowed—and tossed the sacks into the hole. Desperately he began shoveling dirt back in, kicking in stones, anything to fill it before the riders arrived.

Conan put a hand to the leather-wrapped hilt of his broadsword and waited calmly, cool blue eyes watching the hill for the first of the newcomers. They could be anyone, he told himself. They could be concerned with matters other than Malak and himself. But he did not believe it.

II

As a lone horseman in black nasaled helm and gold-chased ebon breastplate crested the hill, Malak laughed shakily. "One man. He may be big, but we can handle one man, if he tries—"

"I heard more than a single horse," Conan said.

"Erlik take them," Malak groaned. Jamming the broken-handled shovel under the edge of a small boulder, he levered the stone toward the hole. "Our horses," he panted. "We can outrun them." The boulder toppled into the narrow pit, plugging it.

Conan snorted, but gave no other answer. The watcher's horse was weighed down with as much armor as its rider, it was true. The two of them would gain a lead, but a short-lived one, he knew.

Their mounts were the sort available on short notice to men who had obvious need of leaving
Shadizar quickly, though each had cost as much in
gems as a king's charger. At a gallop the animals
would founder inside half a league, leaving them
afoot to be run down at their pursuer's leisure.

The watcher had stopped on the crest of the hill.

"What does he wait for?" Malak demanded,
tugging two daggers from his belt. "If we are to
die, I see no reason—"

Abruptly the black-armored warrior raised his
arm, moved it from side to side. Over the hilltop
burst more than fourscore yelling armored riders,
an ebon wave that split to either side of the man
who still sat with upraised arm. At a dead gallop
the warriors roared to the right and left, sweeping
out to encircle Conan and Malak at a distance of
three hundred paces.

"You would think we were an army," Conan
said. "Someone thinks we are dangerous, Malak."

"So many," Malak moaned, and cast a regretful glance at their horses, now whinnying fretfully
and dancing as if they wished to run. He seemed
ready to run with them. "The gold for hiring these
would keep a man in luxury for months. Who
would have thought Amphrates would become so
angry?"

"Perhaps he did not like having his gems stolen,"
Conan said drily.

"We did not take *all* that he had," the wiry
thief muttered. "He could be grateful that some-

thing was left. He could spend a coin or two for incense in the temples, to thank the gods for what remained. He did not have to. . . ."

The Cimmerian was barely aware of his companion's tirade. He had learned long since to listen selectively to the small man, simply no longer hearing Malak's moans of what could have been or should have been, but obviously was not.

At the moment the steely-eyed northlander was intent on four of the encircling warriors, four men who had ridden together and now fumbled with a long bundle one of them bore before his saddle. He glanced back at the hilltop. Another rider, masked, now sat beside the first, watching what occurred below.

Abruptly the tall watcher raised a curled brass horn, like the hunting horns used by nobles. A loud note rang from the hilltop, and the four who had worked at the bundle suddenly unfurled it between them and broke into a gallop, straight for the two men afoot. Four others galloped out to join them.

The big Cimmerian's frown deepened. It was a net they held, and the outriders bore long clubs, as if they would cut off a quarry that sought to evade capture.

Malak took two nervous steps toward the horses.

"Wait." Despite Conan's youth there was a note of command in his voice that stopped the smaller man. "Wait for them, or we are meat for the taking.'' Malak nodded grimly and tightened his grip on his daggers.

Closer the horsemen thundered. A hundred paces. Fifty. Ten. Shouts of triumph broke from the charging warriors.

''Now,'' Conan said, and leaped . . . toward the net. Groaning, Malak followed.

As he leaped, the Cimmerian's broadsword finally left its worn shagreen scabbard. Driven by massive shoulders the blade sheared through a corner of the net. The rider who had held that corner galloped on with a startled yell, holding only a fragment of thick rope. The warrior following behind dropped his reins and drew the curved tulwar at his belt. Conan ducked under the slash, then thrust up, his steel sliding under the black breastplate. The impaled warrior seem to leap backwards from the saddle of his charging horse.

Even as the man fell, Conan tugged free his bloodied steel and spun, warned by a primitive instinct for danger. The face looming above him was twisted with rage beneath the dark helmet's rim, contorted as if the man wished he swung a sword rather than a club. Yet that thick billet, longer than a man's arm, could crack a skull if landed hard enough, and the club-wielder swung with a will. The Cimmerian's blade flashed upward, through flesh and bone. Club and still-clutching hand sailed through the air. As the shrieking man grabbed his scarlet-fountaining wrist with his remaining hand, his horse bolted, carrying him away. Hastily Conan sought for a new enemy.

Malak was grappling with one of the net-carriers, attempting to pull him from the saddle. One of the small thief's daggers darted into the gap between helmet and breastplate. With a gurgling scream the horseman toppled, carrying Malak to the ground with him. The dark-eyed thief bounded quickly to his feet, daggers at the ready. The other man did not move.

For a frozen instant Conan and his companion faced the five remaining of their attackers. The net lay abandoned on the ground, now. The two who had helped bear the net rested their hands on their sword hilts. Those with clubs seemed more hesitant. Suddenly one man threw down his club; before his sword was half drawn another blast of the horn rang out. The sword was resheathed with an oath, and all five galloped back toward the encircling line.

Malak licked his lips. "Why are they trying to capture us? I don't understand."

"Perhaps Amphrates is even madder than we thought," Conan replied grimly. "Perhaps he wants to see how much the Torturers' Guild can make us scream before we die."

"Mitra!" Malak breathed. "Why did you have to tell me something like that?"

Conan shrugged. "You asked." Again the horn sounded. "Get ready. They're coming again."

Again four riders bore the net spread between

them, but this time the outriders brought their number up to a full score. As the horsemen pounded toward them, Conan motioned unobtrusively; Malak shrugged and nodded. The two men stood, waiting, as they had before. Closer the net came, and closer. Only three strides from the men on the ground, half the outriders swung in close to the net. This time there would be no unimpeded cutting of the net or killing of its bearers.

As the outriders closed with the net, Conan leaped to the left and Malak to the right. Net-bearers and outriders galloped between them, cursing and trying to turn their horses. A club swung at Conan's head. Its wielder grunted in surprise when his wrist slapped into the Cimmerian's palm, yelled in disbelief as the massive youth jerked him from the saddle. Conan's fisted hilt struck once, spraying blood and teeth, and his opponent slumped.

Drumming hooves alerted him to an attacker coming from behind. His hand closed on the long club as it fell from nerveless fingers, and he rose, spinning into a backhand blow with the staff. The thick length of wood cracked as it slammed across the midsection of a charging horseman. Eyes bulging and air rushing from him in one long strangled gasp, the rider bent as if seeking to fold himself around the club, and his horse galloped out from under him.

''Conan!''

Before his last opponent had struck the ground Conan was seeking the reason for Malak's cry.

Two of the black-armored warriors were leaning from their saddles to club at a bloody, writhing shape on the ground.

With a wild yell the Cimmerian was on them, ensanguined steel slashing. Two corpses fell away from him as he dragged the small thief to his feet, dazed of eye and with scarlet rivulets streaming down his face. The net-bearers were coming once more, he saw, and Malak was barely able to stand, certainly in no shape to fight.

Muscles bulging in a massive shoulder and arm, Conan hurled his companion aside and leaped for the net. His hand closed on it, and he heaved. A surprised warrior was catapulted from his saddle to land atop the grid of thick ropes, tangling in it as he rolled. A club smashed into the Cimmerian's back, staggering him, but he whirled, roaring, and drove his blade under iron breastplate.

There was no hope of escape. He knew that. Too many men crowded around him, striking with staves and clubs. Dust pounded up by dancing hooves coated his sweated body. The coppery stench of blood was in his nostrils, and his ears were filled with the din of men shouting their rage that he would not fall. Soon he must go down, but he would not surrender. His blade was a whirlwind of razor steel, encarnadining whatever it touched. By fury alone he hacked a way through the press of mounted men, but the mass swirled and enclosed him again.

Loudly the horn sounded, the brazen note slicing through the tumult. And the men who had crowded so about him drew back. With obvious reluctance they abandoned their silent dead and groaning wounded, galloping back to form once more their circle at three hundred paces distance.

In wonder Conan watched them go. Blood trickled in the dust on his face, and stained the back and chest of his tunic. Malak was gone, he saw. No, not gone. Captured. Netted, an arm and a leg sticking through the thick mesh, like a pig on its way to market. Regret coursed through the Cimmerian, and a determination not to end so.

Slowly he turned, attempting to keep an eye on all of those about him. Horses wandered riderless between the circle and him. He might seize one of those and fight his way clear, if he was willing to abandon Malak. He made no move toward a horse. Close to him there were bodies, some still, some twitching. A few cried out for succor, or stretched a hand toward the black-armored watchers.

"Come, then!" Conan shouted at the iron circle. "Let us finish it, an you have the stomach!" Here and there a horse moved as if its rider had shifted angrily, but only silence answered him.

The rattle of rocks sliding down the hill announced the arrival of the two who had remained on the hilltop. The big man in the gold-chased armor stopped at ten paces distance from the Cimmerian, but the leather-masked rider halved that before drawing rein. Conan set himself. He could make out little of the one who approached, for the mask covered all but eyes, and a cloak of black wool swathed all else, but if single combat was sought, Conan was ready.

The lone figure's hands rose to remove the nasaled helmet. Then the mask came off, and the Cimmerian gasped despite himself. A woman faced him, dark eyes smouldering above high cheekbones, raven hair pinned in tight coils about her head. Beautiful she was, with the beauty that can only come to the woman who has left girlhood behind, but there was a fierceness to that beauty, in the firm set to her lovely jaw and the penetrating quality of her gaze. Her cloak was thrown back to reveal riding breeches and tunic of sable silk, clinging to every curve of full breast and rounded thigh. Conan drew a deep breath. Of all women, he had never expected to be confronted by this one.

"You are the one called Conan." Her voice was sensuous, yet imperious.

Conan did not answer. That she had left her perfumed palace and bright gardens for the heat of the plains was surprise enough, but that she had come seeking him—and such he did not now doubt—was more than merely worrisome. Yet he had lived long enough among those who called themselves civilized and him barbarian to know some rules of survival among them. He would give no information until he knew more.

The mounted woman's delicate brows drew down at his silence. "You know who I am, do you not?"

"You are Taramis," Conan replied simply, and her frown deepened.

"Princess Taramis." She emphasized the first word. His face lost none of its grimness, nor did his sword lower from its ready position. She was tall for a woman, and she drew herself up to the last hairsbreadth of her height. "I am the Princess Royal of Zamora. Tiridates, your king, is my brother."

"Tiridates is not *my* king," Conan said.

Taramis smiled as if she found herself back on a familiar path. "Yes," she breathed. "You are a northlander, a barbarian, are you not? And a thief?"

Conan stiffened. It was all he could do not to check the encircling horsemen to see if some were drifting closer with their nets, yet he knew the true danger lay with the woman before him. "What do you want of me?" he demanded.

"Serve me, Conan the thief."

He had had patrons of the moment before, those who gave him gold for a particular theft, and at that moment it seemed his alternative was to battle the remaining black-armored warriors. Yet perversity touched him. "No."

"You refuse me?" Taramis said incredulously.

"I do not like being hunted like an animal. I am no wild boar to be netted."

"I can give you wealth beyond your imaginings, titles and position. You could be a lord in a marble palace instead of a thief in squalid alleys."

Conan shook his head slowly. "You have but

one thing in your gift that I want, and I will not ask it of you.''

''Only one? What is that, barbar?''

''My freedom,'' the Cimmerian smiled. It was the smile of a wolf at bay. ''And that I will take myself.''

The dark-eyed Zamoran princess looked at him wonderingly. ''Do you truly believe you can defeat all of my warriors?''

''Mayhap they can kill me, but that is freedom of another sort, to die rather than yield.''

Still staring, she spoke as if unaware that she did so. ''The scrolls spoke truly.'' Abruptly she shook herself. ''I *will* have you in my service, Conan, and you will ask to enter it.''

The tall warrior in gold-chased armor spoke. ''It is not seemly for you to bargain with his sort. Let me face him, and we will carry him back to Shadizar in a net like his accomplice.''

Without taking her eyes from Conan, Taramis gestured as if waving away a gnat. ''Be silent, Bombatta.''

One hand she stretched toward the Cimmerian, palm out, fingers moving as if she palped something. The air seemed to stir across Conan's broad chest, and he felt the hairs on his arms lift. He found he had taken a step back. Planting his feet, he firmed his grip on his sword hilt.

Taramis' hand dropped, and her eyes went to the crude structure of stones he had built. ''All men have a heart's desire, something they would kill for, or die for." From the neck of her tunic she drew a chain of delicate golden links from which depended a teardrop of clear crystal. The crystal she clasped tightly in her left hand, and her right pointed to the rough altar. "See now what is your seeking, Conan."

From between her fingers closed about the crystal came a pulse of crimson light. Among the encircling warriors horses snorted nervously. Only Taramis' mount was still, although with eyes rolling and flanks trembling. Once more came the flash, and again, and again, until an unceasing glow of purest vermilion shone from her fist.

Suddenly there were flames on the bare stone of the altar, and the warriors' mounts danced and reared in terror. Had Conan sought to flee then, he would have found none opposing, for every rider's whole energy was given to controlling his fear-struck animal, but the big Cimmerian did not even notice them. Among the flames lay a figure, a woman, long blonde hair arranged over her shoulders, firm-muscled body sleekly curved and unblemished.

He clamped his teeth on a name, and muttered instead, "Sorcery!"

"Aye, sorcery." Taramis' voice was soft, but it cut unnaturally through the terrified screaming of the horses. "Sorcery that can give you what you seek, Conan. Valeria."

"She is dead," Conan said roughly. "Dead, and there's an end to it."

"Is it an end, barbar?" Within the fires, the form's head turned. Clear blue eyes gazed into Conan's. The womanly shape sat up, held out a hand to the Cimmerian. "I can give her back to you," Taramis said. "I can return her to this world."

Conan snarled. "As a living corpse? I have encountered such. Better to remain dead."

"No corpse, barbar. Warm flesh. Supple flesh. I can give her to you, and make her as you wish. Would you be certain of her devotion for all time? I can assure it. Would you have her crawl to your feet, worship you as a god? I—"

"No!" The Cimmerian's breath was ragged in this throat. "She was a warrior. I will not have. . . ." He let his hoarse words die.

"So you believe, now?" The dark-eyed woman gestured; the flames and Valeria's image alike vanished, leaving bare, unscorched stone. About her neck the teardrop crystal hung clear once again. "I can do as I say."

Slowly Conan's sword lowered. He had no liking for sorcery, not even when practiced by those mages he knew to have no malign intent, and such were few indeed. But . . . a debt to be repaid. A life freely given in place of his. "Free Malak," he said wearily.

Bombatta sneered. "Having cleaned the streets of Shadizar of a thief, you think we would loose the little scum? He is no use to anyone in this world."

"One thief more or less will make no difference in Shadizar," Conan said, "and he is a friend. Either he goes free, or our further talking will be done with steel."

The huge warrior opened his mouth again, but Taramis silenced him with a look. "Free the little thief," she said quietly.

Bombatta's face was a tight mask of anger and frustration. Viciously he pulled his horse around and galloped to those who guarded the net-wrapped Malak. In moments the ropes had been cut and the wiry man was rolled out on the stony ground.

"They nearly broke my bones," Malak called as he trotted toward Conan. "What was that with the fire? Why are we still ali—?" His eyes fell on Taramis and widened. "Aiiee!" He began to jerk fawning bows, all the while casting frantically questioning looks at the Cimmerian. "We are honest men, O most honored princess, no matter what you may have heard from lying tongues in Shadizar. We . . . hire ourselves out as . . . as caravan guards. Why, never have we taken so much as a pomegranate without payment. You must believe—"

"Begone, little man," Taramis said, "before I tell you how much truth I know of you."

Eying Conan doubtfully, Malak took a hesitant step toward their horses.

"We must part for a time," Conan told him, "even as we did after the fight in the Inn of the Three Crowns. Go, and fare you well."

With a last, helpless look at the surrounding guards, the small man darted for his mount.

When Malak had galloped out of sight over the hill—laying his quirt to his horse and staring back over his shoulder as if he still did not believe he was actually free to go—Conan turned back to Taramis. "What is it you wish me to do?" he asked.

"In good time, you will be told," the beauteous woman replied. The smile that played on her lips was tinged with triumph. "For now, there are words I would hear from you."

Conan did not hesitate. "I would enter your service, Taramis." A debt must be repaid, whatever the cost.

III

Shadizar was a city of golden domes and alabaster spires thrusting toward the cerulean sky from the dust and stones of the Zamoran plain. Crystal pure fountains splashed among fig trees in shaded courtyards, and a glaring sun was reflected from gleaming white walls that sheltered dark cool within. Shadizar the Wicked was the city called, and a score more of names, each less complimentary than the last and all well-earned.

Within the great granite city walls pleasure was sought as avidly as gold, and one was oft exchanged for the other. Sleek lords licked their lips over quivering maidens as over pastries. Hot-eyed ladies stalked their prey like sinuous, sensuous cats. One nobly-born husband and wife, each committed to a life of fleshy delights not encompassing

33

the other, were currently the butt of many jokes, for after intrigues and machinations too involved for recounting they discovered too late that each had managed to arrange an assignation with the other.

Yet if perversion and debauchery were the soul of Shadizar, it was trade that provided the gold to purchase them. From the far reaches of the world they knew came the caravans, from Turan and Corinthia, from Iranistan and Khoraja, from Koth and Shem. Pearls, silks and gold, ivory, perfumes and spices, all provided the music for the licentious pavane of the City of Ten Thousand Sins.

The streets of the city were crowded with commerce as Conan rode into the city with Taramis' party of black-armored warriors. Rough-tunicked men carrying baskets of fruit dodged the whips of muleteers who drove their trains of braying beasts down streets lined with brightly striped shop awnings and tables displaying samples of the goods to be found within. Haughty, silk-clad nobles and fat merchants in somber velvets, leather-aproned apprentices and harlots wearing little but jingling girdles of coin, all dodged between the long-striding camels of caravans driven by dusty men of foreign mien and greedy eyes. From building to building the air was solid with the bleats and squawks of sheep and chickens bound for sale, the cries of peddlers and strumpets hawking their wares, beggars pleading and merchants bargaining. Over all hung a stench compounded of equal parts of spices, offal, perfume and sweat.

Taramis did not allow herself to be slowed by the congestion of the narrow streets. Half of her warriors drove a wedge before her, using the long clubs they still carried to beat aside those who were too slow to clear the way. The rest of the ebon-armored guards brought up the rear, with Conan and Taramis in the middle. And guards they were, the big Cimmerian thought, for all the talk that he had entered the noblewoman's service. He bent from the saddle to scoop a fat pear from a fruitmonger's cart and forced himself to sink into a lazy slouch as he rode, seemingly with no thought but eating the succulent fruit and staring at the crowds.

The teeming throngs of people were driven to the sides of the street, merchants and trulls, nobles and beggars crowded together, trampling blankets of trinkets displayed there, overturning tables before shops. Sullen faces stared at the procession. Bloody faces marked those who had been slow of foot. Most were silent, but the guards just ahead of Taramis shook their clubs at the onlookers and scattered shouts rose of "All hail to the Princess Taramis!" or "The gods' blessings on Princess Taramis!"

Conan's eye fell on a caravan forced into a side-street ahead. The lead camel, people jammed about its feet, jerked continually at the halter-rope held by a slim, dark-skinned man in a dirty turban.

The camels behind, catching its feelings, grunted and shifted nervously.

As Conan rode past the caravan, he tossed aside the core of the pear. Right into the lead camel's nose. With a wild bray the dusty gray beast reared, pulling its halter-rope from the turbanned man's hand. For an instant it seemed not to realize that it was free. Then it bolted, with half a score more camels on its heels, straight through the column of black-armored warriors. The Cimmerian gave his horse its head, and it joined the stampede.

Shouts rose behind him, but Conan bent low over his saddle and let his horse gallop. Scattering peddlers and marketers, the knot of camels, with Conan in its center, rounded a slight bend in the street. The pursuit—there would certainly be pursuit—could not see him, but that shelter could last only moments. He threw himself from the saddle. A heavy blow caught him in the ribs as he rolled beneath the feet of the galloping camels. Then he was springing to his feet, leaping past a staring, open-mouthed tradesman to crouch behind a pile of tight-woven baskets. Hooves pounding the paving stones cleared the street again, and a score of grim-faced warriors in ebon armor thundered by, Bombatta at their head.

Slowly Conan straightened, hitching his swordbelt back into place as the horsemen disappeared down the street. He rubbed at the spot where the camel had kicked him. Camels were malicious beasts, he thought. Not like horses. He had never been able to get along with camels. Abruptly he realized the basket weaver yet stared at him.

"Good baskets," Conan told the man, "but not what I want." The open-mouthed tradesman was still staring when he hurriedly crossed the street and ducked into a narrow alley that stank of urine and rotting garbage.

Down the pinched, twisting alleys the Cimmerian sped, cursing when his feet slid in the slick filth. Whenever he came to a street he paused only long enough to look for men in black nasaled helmets before darting across and into another alley. In a zig-zag pattern he made his way the breadth of Shadizar until, in the shadow of the southern wall of the city, he slipped through the back door of the tavern of Manetes.

The hall inside was dark and cool, though heavy with the smells of bad cooking. Serving girls gave the big Cimmerian startled glances as they hurried to and from the kitchens, for patrons did not ordinarily enter the tavern from the crooked alley behind. Nor did the tall young man with sword and dagger at his belt and blue ice in his eyes look like the usual patron.

In the common room muleteers and camel drivers and carters, outlanders for the most part, filled the tables, the odor of sweat and animals dueling with the smell of sour wine. Supple-hipped doxies in narrow strips of thin, brightly colored silk or less paraded their offerings between the tables scattered across the sand-covered floor. More than one jade eyed the broad-shouldered Cimmerian warmly; some, on the laps of men who had already crossed their palms with silver, earned growls and even cuffs, but the men saved their anger for the wenches. Even those who thought themselves fierce as mastiffs recognized the wolf in the massively muscled youth and directed their thoughts, and their anger, to others than him.

Conan was unaware of the stir he left behind him. Once he was sure the common room held no black-armored warriors he had no interest in who else was there. Swiftly he approached the bar where Manetes held sway.

Tall and thin to the point of boniness, the tavernkeeper's dark eyes were set deep in a cadaverous face. The man's starveling looks did not seem to hurt his custom, however, though Conan had never been able discern why.

"Is Malak here?" Conan asked the innkeeper quietly.

"Top of the stairs," Manetes replied. "Third door on the right." He wiped thin hands on a dirty apron and cast his eyes suspiciously behind the Cimmerian as if looking for pursuit. "Is there trouble in this?"

"Not for you," Conan told him, and headed for the stairs. He had no worries concerning the gaunt-faced man's discretion. There was the matter of saving Manetes' daughter from the clutches of two Iranistanis who had intended her for sale in

Aghrapur. Manetes would keep silent if there were hot irons at his feet.

On the second floor Conan slapped open the indicated door, and jerked back as a slashing dagger barely missed his throat. " 'Tis me, you fool!" he growled.

Grinning nervously, Malak sheathed his blade and backed into the room. Conan slammed the door behind him as he entered.

"Sorry," the wiry thief laughed shakily. "It's just . . . well . . . Mitra's Mercies, Conan, Taramis herself out there hunting us, and that fire—that was sorcery, was it not?—and I did not know what had happened to you, and. . . . How did you get free? I'd almost forgotten the fight at the Inn of the Three Crowns, and meeting here after. Do we leave the city now? Did they dig up the gems? We'll go there first thing and dig them up ourselves. Those stones will keep us—"

"Calm yourself," Conan said. "We are not leaving Shadizar. At least, not yet. I have a commission from Taramis."

"What kind of commission?" Malak asked warily. "And how much gold is she offering?"

"What she wants, I don't know yet. As for price . . . Taramis claims she can bring Valeria back."

The smaller man's breath hissed in through clenched teeth. His dark eyes darted as if looking for a way out. "Sorcery," he managed at last. "I *knew* that fire was sorcery. But do you think she has *that* much power? And even if she does, can you trust her?''

''I must take the chance, for Valeria. I owe. . . .'' He shook his head. Malak was a friend, but he would not understand. ''You have no such reason, so I will give you my half of Abulates' gems if you will help me.''

Malak brightened immediately. ''You did not not have to make this offer, Cimmerian. We are companions, eh? Still, I will accept it, just so everything is fair. That is, so long as I don't have to enter Taramis' palace. She put three of my cousins in her dungeon a few years gone, and two of them died there.''

''She doesn't know you from Hannuman's goose-girl, Malak. Still, I will not ask it of you, and you can be sure Taramis won't. On the plain all she wanted of you was that you leave.''

''That just shows how little she knows of talent,'' the small thief huffed. ''If she wants a thief, who is better than me? What am I saying? I'll burn incense in Mitra's temple to give thanks that she chose you rather than me. What do you want me to do?''

''I will go to Taramis' palace. You watch it carefully. I do not know where I may have to go, and I may not have time to seek you out first if I must leave the city. Also, find out where Akiro is.''

''Another sorcerer?'' Malak exclaimed.

A sorcerer, indeed, was Akiro. A short, plump

man with yellow skin like the men of far Khitai, though he had never named any land as his place of birth, he had aided Conan once before with his powers. The Cimmerian did not trust him, entirely—he did not truly trust any wizard—but Akiro had liked Valeria. Perhaps that would weigh in the balance.

"I may have need of him in this, Malak, to watch Taramis' sorceries, to make sure Valeria is not returned with some bond-spell on her."

"I will find him, Cimmerian. Do you have time for a drink to luck, or must you return to Taramis' palace immediately?"

"I must go there for the first time," Conan laughed. "I left her company without farewells, and her guards scour the streets for me. But I hope to reach the palace without killing any of them."

Malak shook his head. "You will be lucky if she is not angry enough to have a pike decorated with your head."

"She may be angry enough, but she will not do it. She sought not just any thief, Malak, but me. She knew my name, and she rode onto the plain to find me. Whatever she intends, Conan of Cimmeria is necessary to it."

IV

To the city that surrounded it, the palace of Taramis presented the look of a fortress, though not, of course, so much a one as the Royal Palace. That would have been a good way to be shortened a head, drunkard though Tiridates might be. Taramis' crenellated granite walls stood four times the height of a tall man, being thus two paces shorter than those of the King. Square towers stood at the four corners of the walls, and two more flanked the tall, iron-bound gates.

Those gates stood open as Conan approached, guarded by two warriors in nasaled helms and black breastplates, with long-bladed spears slanted smartly. Other pairs stood, as rigid as the stone they guarded, atop the towers, and more along the walls. The big Cimmerian's lip curled in contempt for such guards. Like statues, they were, and as much use. On a moonlit night a blind thief could find his way between them without being seen.

The sun now dropped toward the western horizon, and the guards at the massive gates were near the end of their watch, bored and with their minds filled with the food and wine and serving girls that awaited them in their barracks. Conan was within three paces before they realized that he truly meant to enter rather than merely pass by. In their experience, men such as he did not enter the palace of the Princess Royal unless on their way to her dungeons. Their spears dropped as one, long points presented to his chest.

"Be off with you," one of them growled.

"I am here to see Taramis," Conan announced.

Their eyes ran over the sweat-caked dust that covered him, and sneers painted their faces. He who had spoken before opened his mouth. "You were told to—"

Suddenly Bombatta was there, flinging a guard to either side as if he barely noticed they had been in his way. The guards slammed against the thick, iron-bound planks of the open gates and collapsed groggily. Bombatta stood where they had been, glaring at Conan, his hand opening and closing on his sword hilt.

"You dare come here after—?" The massive scar-faced warrior drew a shuddering breath. His black eyes were on a level with Conan's. "Where in Zandru's Nine Hells did you get to?"

"The camels frightened my horse," Conan said carelessly. "Besides, I needed a tankard or two of wine to clear the dust from my throat after the ride back to Shadizar."

Bombatta ground his teeth. "Come with me," he snapped, spinning to reenter the palace. The guards, just now rising to their feet, stayed carefully out of his way, but he shouted, "Togra! Replace those buffoons at the gate!" as soon as he was inside the walls.

Conan followed, but he was no lackey to hurry after the other, as he must were he to catch up. Instead he took his own pace, ignoring Bombatta's darkening face as he had to slow his own steps or leave the Cimmerian behind.

A broad, flagstoned way led from the gate to the palace proper through an elaborate garden where marble fountains splashed and shimmered with watery mists and alabaster spires rose to treble the height of the outer wall. Here tall trees cast a pool of gentle shade. There open spaces were filled with flowering shrubs and plants brought from as far as Vendhya and Zingara. Formal walks laced through it all, and merely within Conan's sight half a score gardeners, their short tunics and bare legs marking them slave, labored to increase its beauty.

A portico of tall fluted columns surrounded the palace itself, and within was a profusion of courtyards floored with polished marble and overlooked by balconies piercing niveous walls that gleamed even in the fading light. Tapestries of wondrous workmanship draped the corridors, and fine carpets from Vendhya were strewn in profusion. Slaves scurried to light golden lamps against the coming night.

Ever inward Bombatta led, until Conan wondered if he were being taken through the entire palace. Then he entered a courtyard and stopped, neither noticing nor caring that the other man had stopped as well. Pedestals stood about the court, on each a symbol carved in alabaster or porphyry or obsidian. Some he recognized from the charts of astrologers. Others he was glad he did not know; his gaze did not linger on those. Among the pedestals stood knots of men in robes of saffron and black, embroidered with arcane signs in varying degrees of complexity. Others, in robes of gold, held to themselves apart. All their eyes swung to him as he stepped into the court, eager eyes, eyes that weighed and measured and evaluated.

"The man Conan," Bombatta said, and the Cimmerian realized he addressed not the watching men, but Taramis, on a balcony overlooking them all.

The voluptuous noblewoman still wore her travel-stained garments, and her face was filled with arrogant fury. Her eyes locked with Conan's. She seemed to be waiting for him to look away, and when he did not, her head jerked irritably. "Have him washed," she commanded, "and brought to me." Without another word she left the balcony, even her back eloquent of rage.

Her anger was no greater than Conan's own, however. *"Have* me washed!" he growled. "I am no horse!" To his surprise, Bombatta's scarred face reflected his ire.

"The baths are this way, thief!" The ebon-armored man all but snarled the words, and strode off, not looking to see if Conan followed.

The Cimmerian hesitated only a moment, though. He would welcome the chance to sluice away the dust; it was only the means of its offering—if it could be called an offer—that rankled.

The room to which Conan was led had walls mosaicked in images of blue skies and river rushes, and in its center was a large, white-tiled pool. Beyond the pool was a low couch and a small table bearing vials of oils. It was the bath-attendants who brought a smile to his face, though. Four girls flashed dark-eyed glances at him and hid giggles behind their hands. Their hair was uniformly black and pinned in identical coils tight about their heads, but short tunics of white linen fit snugly over curves that ranged from slender to generous.

"You will be sent for, thief," Bombatta said.

Conan's smile faded. "Your tone begins to grate at me," he said coolly.

"If you were not needed. . . ."

"Do not let that stay your hand. I shall still be here . . . after."

Bombatta's hand twitched toward his sword; then, the scars on his face livid, he stalked from the chamber.

The four girls had fallen silent during the exchange. Now they huddled together, staring at Conan with frightened eyes.

"I will not bite you," Conan told them gently.

Hesitantly they moved to him, simultaneously beginning to tug at his garments and chatter.

"I thought you were going to fight him, my lord."

"Bombatta is a fierce warrior, my lord. A dangerous man."

"Of course, my lord, you are as tall as he. I thought no man could be as tall as Bombatta."

"But Bombatta is bigger. Not that I doubt your strength, my lord."

"Hold," Conan laughed, fending them off. "One at a time. Firstly, I am no lord. Secondly, I can wash myself. And thirdly, how are you called?"

"I am Aniya, my lord," the slenderest of them answered. "These are Taphis, Anouk and Lyella. And to wash you is what we are for, my lord."

Conan ran an appreciative eye over her lithe curves. "I can think of better things," he murmured. To his surprise Aniya blushed deeply.

"It—it is forbidden, my lord," she stammered. "We are sealed to the Sleeping God." Gasps came from the other three, and Aniya's face paled as quickly as it had colored.

"The sleeping god?" Conan said. "What god is that?"

"Please, my lord," Aniya moaned, "it must

not be spoken of. Please. If you reveal what I have said, I . . . I will be punished.''

"I will hold my silence," Conan promised. But for all he said, they would speak no further word that did not concern his bathing.

He held still for being soaped and rinsed, then soaped and rinsed again. They dried him with soft toweling, then massaged fragrant oils into his skin. Not the most fragrant, to be sure. He managed to avoid those, though he still thought he smelled as perfumed as a noble fop by the time they were done. They were dressing him in robes of white silk when a bald and wizened man entered.

"I am Jarvaneus," the old man said, bowing slightly, "Chief Steward to the Princess Taramis." His tone indicated he considered that position infinitely higher than that of a thief. "If you are finished, I will take you to—" He coughed as Conan took up his sword belt. "There is no need for that here."

Conan fastened the belt and settled the broadsword and dagger into place. He had little liking of being unarmed in any circumstances, and the more he learned the less he wanted to be so in Taramis' palace. "Take me to Taramis," he said.

Jarvaneus choked. "I will take you to the *Princess* Taramis."

The Cimmerian waved him to lead on.

Surprise upon surprise, Conan thought when the old man left him. It was no audience chamber he had been taken to. Golden lamps gave light against the deepening night. A huge, round bed veiled with sheer, white silk took up one end of the great room. The marble-tiled floor was strewn with rugs from Vendhya and Iranistan, and in its center stood a low table of polished brass on which rested a crystal flagon of wine and two goblets of beaten gold. Taramis, swathed in black silk robes from neck to toe, reclined on cushions piled beside the table.

They were not alone in the room. In each corner stood a black-armored warrior, unhelmeted and with his sword slung across his back so that the hilt stuck above his right shoulder. Straight ahead these men stared, not moving a muscle, not seeming to breathe or to blink.

"My bodyguards," Taramis said, gesturing to the four. "The best of Bombatta's warriors, almost as good as he himself. But do not let them worry you. They attack only at my command. Wine?"

She rose smoothly and bent to fill the goblets. Conan's breath caught in his throat. The black silk had tightened across her rounded buttocks as she bent. In its multitude of folds, the garment was opaque, but in a single layer it was as mist. And Taramis wore naught beneath it but sleek skin. As she came toward him with the wine, he found he could not take his eyes from the slight sway of her heavy breasts.

"I said, if you wish food, I will have something

brought for you." The noblewoman's voice was thick with amusement.

Conan started, colored, then colored deeper when he realized what he had done. "No. No, I want nothing to eat." Furious with himself, he took a goblet. What was he about, he wondered, staring like a boy who had never seen a woman before. If he could not keep his wits better than that, he had as well give it over. He cleared his throat. "There is a commission you want me to carry out. I cannot do it until I know what it is."

"You want this Valeria returned to you?" She moved closer, till her breasts brushed against his chest. Even through his tunic they seemed to burn like two hot coals.

"I want her alive again." He stepped to the cushions—casually, he hoped—and lay back. Taramis came to stand over him; he looked up, and had to pull his eyes away from the tantalizing line of thigh and belly and breast. He did not see the small smile that flashed across her lips.

"Hold hard in your mind to what you want, thief, and do as I command."

"You still have not told me what I must do." He had to suppress a sigh of relief when she moved away from him and began to pace.

"I have a niece, the Lady Jehnna," Taramis said slowly. "She has lived her life in seclusion. Her parents, my brother and his wife, died when she was little more than an infant. The shock was too much for her. The child is . . . delicate, her mind fragile. But now she must go on a journey, and you must accompany her.''

Conan choked on a mouthful of wine. "*I* must accompany her?" he said when he had his breath back. "I am not accustomed to being a companion to noblewomen. I mean, it is not the sort of thing I do."

"You mean you are a thief," Taramis said, and smiled when he shifted uncomfortably. "I have not turned you over to the City Guard yet, Conan. Why should I now? It is a thief I need, for Jehnna must steal a key, a key only she can touch, and also the treasure that key will open the way to for her. Who better to aid her in that than the best thief in Zamora?"

The big youth felt as though his head was spinning. Carefully he set the goblet on the table. The last thing he needed then was wine. "I am to take this child, this Lady Jehnna, on a journey, and help her steal an ensorceled key and a treasure," he said wonderingly. "If you say this is the service you require in return for Valeria, I will do it, though I cannot see why she does not travel with a retinue of servants and a hundred of your guards instead of with one thief."

"Because the Scrolls of Skelos say she must journey without such." Taramis stopped, biting at her lower lip.

"These scrolls," he began, but the silk-draped woman waved a quick hand in dismissal.

"Prophecies," she said hastily. "They tell what

must be done, and how. Put them from your mind. They are in an ancient tongue known only to . . . scholars.'' She eyed him consideringly, then went on. ''There is some vagueness about numbers, but only two companions are mentioned specifically. I have decided to risk sending no more than that. The two will be yourself and Bombatta.''

Conan grunted, abandoning the scrolls for more immediate concerns. Bombatta to ride with him? Well, he would deal with the man when and if he had to. ''Where is this key to be found?''

''The Lady Jehnna will show you.''

''It will be best if I have a map,'' he told her, ''and a plan of the place where the key is kept. The treasure, too. And what manner of treasure is it? Will we need pack animals to carry it?''

''The Lady Jehnna will know it when she sees it, my fine thief. And she can hold it in her hands, which no one else can do. That is all you need to know. As for a map, there is none, can be none, outside of Jehnna's head. At her birth spells were cast to attune her to this key. She will sense the key as you journey, and know how to reach it. When the key is her hand, she will become attuned to the treasure in the same way.''

Conan sighed. That she wished to keep some things secret from him was no surprise. Many patrons found it hard to completely trust a thief, even when he was in their hire. Still, it did not make matters easier. ''Is there aught else I should know, or prepare for? Remember that too many surprises may mean not only my death, but that of your niece.''

"Jehnna must not be harmed!" Taramis snapped.

"I will keep her safe, but I cannot do it in complete ignorance. If you know something more. . . .''

"Very well. I . . . am reliably informed that the key is now in the possession of a man called Amon-Rama, a Stygian.''

"A sorcerer." He could not believe otherwise, after all else he had heard.

"Aye, a sorcerer. You see, I tell you everything that I know. I wish success for this journey as much or more than you. Are you frightened, or can you face what comes? Remember your Valeria.''

His face hardened at her words. "I have said I will do it, and I will.''

"Very well," Taramis said. "Now, one final thing, as important as all the rest, at least to you. On the seventh night from now will there be a configuration of the stars that occurs but once in a thousand years. It is during that configuration that I can bring Valeria back to you. *If* you have returned to me with the treasure and the Lady Jehnna.'' Her raised hand forestalled the protest he was forming. "My astrologers can locate neither the key nor the treasure, but they assure me both can be found and returned here within the time.''

"They assure you," he laughed grimly.

He peered into his goblet, and drained the rest of the wine in one gulp. An hour before, he thought, he had waded to his knees in sorcery, and cautiously. Now he knew he waded to his neck, and in the fog.

Suddenly a scream ripped through the palace, a girl's scream. Again it came, and again. Conan leaped to his feet, a hand going to his sword. He saw the guards tense, and realized it was in response to him. The screams had brought no stir from them.

"It is my niece," Taramis said hastily. "Jehnna suffers nightmares. Sit, Conan. Sit. I will return when I have seen to her comfort." And to the Cimmerian's surprise the Princess Royal of Zamora ran from the room.

Taramis did not not have far to run, and anger lent her speed. She had thought the nightmares dealt with, gone to plague their nights no more. Her niece was curled into a ball in the middle of her bed, sobbing convulsively in the dim light of the moon shining through arched windows. Taramis was not surprised to find no servant in attendance. They knew only she could deal with the dark visions that tormented Jehnna's night. The noblewoman knelt beside the bed and put her hands on Jehnna's shoulders.

The girl started, then saw Taramis and clutched at her. "It was a dream!" she wept. "A horrible dream!" Not yet eighteen, Jehnna was slender and pretty, but now her large, dark eyes swam with tears and her full lips trembled beyond control.

"Only a dream," Taramis soothed, stroking the girl's long, black hair. "No more than a dream."

"But I saw—I saw—"

"Ssssh. Rest, Jehnna. Tomorrow you begin your grand adventure. You cannot let dreams frighten you now."

"But it frightened me so," Jehnna faltered.

"Hush, child."

Lightly Taramis rested her fingertips on Jehnna's temples, and chanted beneath her breath. Slowly the girl's sobs quieted, her tremblings stilled. When her breathing took on the slow, deep rhythm of sleep, Taramis straightened. A hundred times she had thought the dream and the memories of the dream were banished, but each time the accursed dream returned to haunt her. She rubbed at her own temples. The same power that gave the girl her destiny made it harder each time to push away the nightmare. But without that power and destiny there would have been no nightmares. Jehnna was the One spoken of in the scrolls, and that was what was important. This time the banishment would last long enough. It had to.

All of her life had Taramis been on this path, truly since infancy. As soon as she was old enough to be aware of herself, her own aunt, the Princess Elfaine, began to teach her of the only two ways a woman could truly have power, seduction and sorcery. When Elfaine died, the child Taramis, but ten years of age, did not attend the funereal rites. Older heads thought her absence was an indication of her grief. In actuality she had been ransacking her aunt's private chambers, stealing the sorcerous tomes and magical artifacts that Elfaine had spent a lifetime collecting. And there she found the Scrolls of Skelos. Within a phasing of the moon she began the twenty years of labor that now approached culmination.

She became aware of Bombatta standing in the doorway, staring at the girl on the bed. Swiftly she crossed the room and took him by the arms. For a moment he resisted; then he allowed himself to be drawn into the darkened corridor.

"You no longer even hide it, do you?" she said with deceptive quiet. "You desire my niece. Do not attempt to deny it."

He towered over her, but he shifted from foot to foot like a boy awaiting chastisement. "I cannot help myself," he muttered finally. "You are fire and passion. She is innocence and purity. I cannot help myself."

"And she must remain innocent. It is written in the Scrolls of Skelos."

In truth, the scrolls did not require Jehnna to be virgin, merely innocent of the slightest seed of evil, a pure soul incapable of thinking wrong or harm toward anyone or of believing that anyone might mean such toward her. Her carefully cloistered life had assured that. But Taramis had seen what was happening in Bombatta long before he had become aware of it himself, and nurtured his belief.

"Even were it not," she told him, "you are mine, and I will not share what is mine."

"I like it not that you are alone with the thief," he growled.

"Alone?" Taramis laughed. "The four best of your guards stand ready to seize him or cut him down should he threaten me." The huge warrior spoke under his breath, and she frowned. "Speak loudly enough for me to hear, Bombatta. I do not like things hidden from me."

For a long moment he stared at her, black eyes burning, then said, "I cannot bear the thought of the thief looking at you, wanting you, touching you. . . ."

"You forget yourself." Each word slashed like an icy razor. Bombatta took a step back, then slowly sank to his knees, head bent.

"Forgive me," he muttered. "But this Conan cannot be trusted. He is an outlander, a thief."

"Fool! The scrolls say that Jehnna must be accompanied by a thief with eyes the color of the sky. There is not another such in Shadizar, perhaps not in all of Zamora. You will do as I have commanded you. You will follow the instruction of the scrolls exactly. Exactly, Bombatta."

"As you command," he murmured, "so do I obey."

Taramis touched his head, much as she might fondle the head of one of her wolfhounds. "Of course, Bombatta." She felt flushed with victory, for it certainly would come now. The Horn of

Dagoth would be hers. Immortality and power would be hers. The knowledge sent sparks through her, and flashes of heat that coiled in her belly. Her hand trembled on Bombatta's black hair. She took a deep breath. "Rest assured that all will occur as I have planned, Bombatta. Now return to your chambers and sleep. Sleep, and dream of our triumph."

Unmoving on his knees, Bombatta watched her go, his obsidian eyes glittering in the dark.

Conan got to his feet as Taramis entered the bedchamber. "Your niece?" he asked.

"She is better. She sleeps." The voluptuous noblewoman raised a hand, and the ebon-clad guards marched from the room without a word. "Do *you* sleep, thief, or are you awake? It is late, and you would talk of my niece." Folds of diaphanous silk moved as she walked, showing flashes of bare skin beneath.

The Cimmerian eyed her doubtfully. With a serving girl or even a rich merchant's daughter, he would have been certain what she meant. With a princess he was unsure.

"Are you still a man?" she laughed. "Has mourning for your beloved Valeria unmanned you?"

Conan growled. He knew he could not explain to Taramis what had stood and did stand between Valeria and himself. He was not sure he had it entirely clear in his own mind. But of one thing he was sure. "I am a man," he said.

Taramis' hands went to her neck. Black silk cascaded to pool about her feet. There was challenge in her dark eyes, and her rounded nudity. "Prove it," she taunted.

Disdaining the bed, Conan bore her to the floor and gave the proofs she asked.

D

Conan stared into the fire of dried dung—small, so as to attract no unwanted attention from others who might be spending the night on the Zamoran plain—and thought briefly of other, sorcerous flames on a crude stone altar. A full day's ride from Shadizar, and still Malak had not appeared. The Cimmerian did not like admitting to a need for anyone's aid, but he was more certain than ever that he would need Akiro before this journey was done. And after, if Taramis delivered what she promised. Where in Zandru's Nine Hells was Malak?

Scowling, he pulled himself from the useless reverie and found himself studying his companions. Or rather, one of them.

Bombatta solicitously filled a silver cup from

one of their goatskin waterbags and offered it to
Jehnna. With a thankful smile she reached one
hand from under her cloak of the palest white
wool, pulled tight about her against the chill of the
night. The girl was not at all what Conan expected,
and he still had not accustomed himself to the
difference. Taramis had spoken of her niece as a
child, and he had formed an image of a girl of nine
or ten years, not one of his own age, with a
slender body that moved beneath her concealing
robes with the unconscious grace of a gazelle.

"Our direction," the Cimmerian said abruptly.
"Do we continue the same way on the morn,
Jehnna?"

"The Lady Jehnna, thief," Bombatta corrected
in a growl.

Jehnna blinked, as if startled at being addressed.
Her brown eyes, as large and tremulous as those of
a newborn fawn, stared at him for a moment, then
turned to Bombatta. She addressed her answer to
the black-armored warrior. "I will know more
later, but for now, I know only that we must ride
to the west."

Toward the Karpash Mountains, Conan thought.
They were a rugged, towering range where a man
could easily become lost if he had neither a famil-
iarity with the region nor a guide with the same.
Maps showed only the major passes, used as trade
routes. And the people, if not so fierce as Ke-
zankian hillmen, were yet far from friendly toward

strangers. They had a way of smiling in welcome until they put the knife into your ribs.

The Cimmerian was not surprised that she had not answered him directly. Since leaving Taramis' palace before dawn she had spoken no word to him, only to Bombatta. But he was skilled in his chosen profession, and knowledge was as life's blood to a thief. "How do you know the way?" he asked. "Does the key draw you to it?"

"She is not to be questioned, thief," Bombatta growled.

A wolf howled in the night, the long, mournful sound seeming to blend with the crescent-mooned darkness.

"What was that, Bombatta?" Jehnna asked curiously.

The scar-faced man gave a last glare to Conan before replying. "Only an animal, child. Like a dog."

Her brown eyes turned eager. "Will we see one?"

"Perhaps, child."

Conan shook his head. The girl seemed to delight in everything, and to know of nothing. The empty streets of Shadizar as they rode from the city, the tents and sleeping camels of a caravan outside the city gates, the pack of hyenas that had followed them at a distance for half the day without ever quite gathering the nerve to attack, all fascinated her equally, bringing bright-eyed stares and questions to Bombatta.

"What I do not know can kill us," Conan said.

"Do not frighten her, thief!" Bombatta snapped.

Jehnna laid a hand on the tall warrior's chain-mailed arm. "I am not frightened, Bombatta. My good Bombatta."

"Then tell me how you know where to find the key," Conan insisted. "Or tell Bombatta, if you still will not speak to me."

Her eyes flickered to Conan, then settled on a space halfway between the Cimmerian and the black-armored warrior. "I do not *know* exactly how I know the way, only that I do. It is as if I remember having been this way before." She shook her head and gave a small laugh. "Of course, it cannot be that. I do not in truth remember ever having left the palace of my aunt until this day."

"If you can tell me where we are to go," Conan said, "even if only vaguely, I may be able to take us by a shorter route than the one you know." Thinking of the configuration of stars Taramis had said was necessary for restoring Valeria to life, he touched the golden amulet hanging at his neck and added, "Time is short."

Once more Jehnna gave a slight shake of her head. "If what I see before me is the proper way to go, then I . . . remember it. But I must see it first." Abruptly she laughed and let herself fall back to stare up at the sky. "Besides, I do not want this journey to end quickly. I wish it could last forever and ever."

"It cannot, child," Bombatta said. "We must be back in Shadizar in six more nights."

It was all Conan could do to keep his face expressionless. The configuration would occur in six nights, but Bombatta had no care for Valeria's return. What else was to occur on that night?

"Now it is time for you to sleep, girl," the scarred man went on. "We must travel onward early." He began preparing her bed, clearing rocks away from a space of ground, then digging at the earth with his dagger.

"Please, Bombatta," Jehnna said, "can I not remain awake a little longer? The stars look so different here than from the palace gardens. It seems I could almost touch them." Bombatta wordlessly spread blankets over the softened ground. "Oh, very well," she sighed, then covered a yawn with her hand. "It's just that I want to experience everything, and there is so much."

As she lay down, Bombatta put another blanket over her with surprising gentleness. "I will let you experience as much as I can," he said softly. "As much as I can, child, but we must be back in Shadizar in six nights more."

Pillowing her head on her arms, Jehnna mumbled sleepily.

A lover, Conan thought, watching the way Bombatta remained bent over the girl. Were Jehnna not so obviously a virgin he would have been sure the other man was her lover.

Rising to his feet, Bombatta walked to the fire

and began to kick dirt over it. "I will take the first watch, thief," he said. Without another word he returned to Jehnna's side, drew his sword, and sat crosslegged with the naked blade across his knees.

Conan's mouth tightened. The man had placed himself between Jehnna and the Cimmerian, as if it were he who must be guarded against. Not taking his eyes from Bombatta, Conan stretched out on the ground, one hand gripping his own swordhilt. He drew no blanket over himself. He was inured to more cold than the Zamoran plain had to offer, and a blanket would slow him an instant should he need to bring his sword into play. Such could be fatal against a man with steel already in his fist. Yet even through his distrust of Bombatta, he wondered about the new mystery that had been added to the rest. What was to occur in Shadizar in six nights? His mind was still on that when he allowed sleep to overtake him.

The rufescent sun beat down fiercely on the mounted trio making their way westward across the Zamoran plains, and Jehnna tugged the hood of her snowy cloak lower in a vain attempt to find coolness in its shadow on her face. She knew Bombatta was right when he said the cloak protected her from the sun—she had held a hand out from under the cloak long enough to feel the strength of the sun's direct rays, and been convinced—but that did not lessen the heat. This was one experience she felt she could do without. Ahead loomed the gray bulk of snow-capped mountains, the Karpash Mountains, promising both cool and wetness. She licked her lips, but they were dry almost as she was done.

"The mountains, Bombatta," she said. "We shall reach them soon?"

He turned toward her, and a thrill of fear shot through her at his scarred, sweaty visage in the ebon helmet. Foolishness, she told herself. To be afraid of Bombatta, whom she had known all of her life? Foolishness indeed.

"Not soon, child," he replied. "Tomorrow. In the morning, perhaps."

"But they seem so near," she protested.

"It is the air of the plains, child. Distances seem nothing to the eye. The mountains are many leagues distant yet."

Jehnna thought of asking for another drink of water, but she had seen Bombatta eyeing the waterskins after her last drink, weighing what remained. He had taken only two drinks since waking. Her eyes went to Conan, leading them, with the packhorse's rope tied to his saddle. The northlander had taken one swallow of water on waking and had not looked at the waterbags since. Now he rode easily, one hand resting lightly on his sword hilt, eyes always searching ahead, apparently not even noticing that the sun had broiled them since dawn and was still not halfway to its zenith.

What a strange young man he was, she thought,

though she had little with which to make comparison. He was no older than her, she was sure, but his eyes—such a peculiar color for eyes, blue—seemed unimaginably older. Thirst did not bother him, nor the heat. Could anything slow him? Rain, or wind, or snow? She had heard stories about snow in the mountains, piled as high as a palace. No, she was certain he would go on, deterred by nothing. Perhaps that was why her aunt had sent him. Perhaps he was a hero, a prince in disguise, as in the stories some of the serving girls told her when her aunt was not there.

She shot a glance at Bombatta from the corner of her eye. "Is he handsome, Bombatta?"

"Is who handsome?" he asked gruffly.

"Conan."

His head swiveled toward her; for an instant she was afraid again. "You should not think of such things." His voice was hard, with no trace of the gentleness he usually had with her. "Especially not about him."

"Do not be mad at me, Bombatta," she pleaded. "I love you, and I do not want you to ever be angry with me."

A pained look flashed across his face. "I . . . love you, too, Jehnna. I am not angry with you. It is just that. . . . Do not think about the thief. Put him from your mind entirely. That is best."

"I do not see how I can do that, when he rides with us. Besides, Bombatta, I think perhaps he *is* handsome, as in the stories about princes."

"He is no prince," Bombatta snorted.

Jehnna felt a flash of disappointment, but went on. "Even so, I think he is. Handsome, I mean. But I have no one to compare him with, save you and the male slaves and servants in Taramis' palace, and I cannot see any of them as handsome. They are always kneeling and bowing and groveling." Bombatta's face had been growing harder as she spoke; she hunted among her words for something that might have offended him. "Oh, of course you are handsome, Bombatta. I did not mean to imply that you are not."

The big man's teeth ground audibly. "I told you not to think of such things."

"He is bigger than any of the slaves. He's almost as big as you, Bombatta. Do you think he is as strong as you? Perhaps that is why Taramis sent him with us, because he is as strong as you, and as brave as you, and as great a warrior."

"Jehnna!"

She jumped in her saddle, and stared. He had never shouted at her before. Never.

Breathing hard, he rode with one fist on his hip. staring straight ahead. Finally he said, "This Conan is a thief, child. Only a thief, and no more. The Princess Taramis had her own reasons for sending him with us. It is not for me to question them, nor for you."

Jehnna chewed at her lip as she mulled over what she had just learned. When Taramis told her the day for her journey had come, she had been overjoyed. It meant the fullfilling of her destiny. She would find the Horn of Dagoth and return it to her aunt, and great honor would be bestowed on her. But if Conan was a thief, and Taramis had sent him with them. . . .

"Bombatta, are we going to *steal* the Horn of Dagoth?"

He made a chopping motion with his hand, and looked quickly toward Conan. The blue-eyed young giant still rode before them, too far ahead to hear words that were not shouted. From the stiffness of his back Jehnna thought he was deliberately ignoring Bombatta and her. For some reason she did not quite understand, it annoyed her that he might ignore her. And on purpose.

"Child," Bombatta said quietly, "Taramis told you not to mention that name in the hearing of anyone but her or me. You know that. It is our secret."

"He cannot hear us," she protested. "And *are* we going to—"

"No!" His tone became overly patient, the way it did when she had pushed him to a limit. "No, Jehnna, we do not steal. No one save you can touch the key. No one save you can touch the Horn. No one in the entire world. Is that not proof that your destiny is true? You cannot doubt your aunt, or me."

"Of course not, Bombatta. It is just . . . oh, I'm sorry. I did not mean to make a bother." The scar-faced warrior muttered something angrily under his breath; she stared at him. "What, Bombatta?"

Instead of answering, he galloped ahead of her, toward Conan.

She stared after him, and abruptly realized someone had ridden over a hill to the north of them and was fast approaching, leading another horse behind him on a rope. He was an ugly little man, she saw as he came closer, short and wiry, in a leather jerkin and dirty breeches. Suddenly her mind puzzled out what it was that Bombatta had muttered. Malak, he had said.

Conan permitted himself a grin when Malak appeared, riding across the hilltop, a saddled horse behind him on a lead rope. He shifted the smooth pebble he was using to bring moisture to his mouth from under his tongue to his cheek. "Ho, Malak!" he called.

"Ho, Conan!" A broad grin split the wiry thief's face. "I had a hard time finding you, Cimmerian. I am no tracker, you know. I am a man of the cities, a civilized—"

Bombatta cut between the two of them, reining in with a spray of dust and rocks. He ignored Conan to glare at the small man, whose smile faded slowly under that murderous gaze.

"The Princess Taramis gave you your life," Bombatta snarled. "You should have lost yourself in a pigsty while you had the chance."

"I asked him to come," Conan said.

Bombatta pulled his horse around, his scars livid lines across his face. "*You* asked him! What made you think you could decide who came on this journey, thief? The Princess Taramis—"

"Taramis wants me to accompany Jehnna," Conan cut him off, "and I want Malak."

"And I say no!"

Conan took a deep breath. He would remain calm. He would not kill this fool. "Then continue the quest without me," he said with more coolness than he felt.

It was Bombatta's turn to take a deep breath. His teeth grated, though, as he failed in showing the same outward equilibrium as the Cimmerian. "There are reasons, thief, that you cannot know. You and I and the Lady Jehnna must go on alone."

"Taramis said the numbers were vague," Conan said, and was pleased to see the other's face go slack with surprise.

"She told you that?"

Conan nodded. "Taramis does not want us to fail. She told me everything."

"Of course," Bombatta said slowly, but there was that about his tone that suddenly made Conan doubt his own words. Yet surely she would not have kept anything back if that would hinder their chances for success.

"Well?" Conan said. "Does Malak ride with us, or do he and I go our own way?"

Bombatta's hand tightened on his sword hilt until his knuckles paled. "Keep the little wretch, then," he breathed hoarsely. "But make no mistake, thief. If we fail because of him, I'll slice both of you for dog meat. And keep a proper respect about you for the Princess Taramis and the Lady Jehnna!" Sawing at his reins, he galloped back to Jehnna, who sat her horse watching worriedly.

"I do not think that man likes me," Malak laughed weakly.

"You have survived other men who did not like you," Conan replied. "You will survive Bombatta. A sorry beast," he added, then gestured to Malak's spare horse when the small man raised a questioning eyebrow.

Malak chuckled. "It was all I could steal. It's for Akiro."

"Is he close? I have no time to seek him very far."

"Not far. The way you're traveling, and to the south."

"Then we must ride," Conan said. "Time is lacking."

Malak fell in beside him as he started forward again. The Cimmerian twisted in his high-pommeled saddle to make sure Bombatta and the girl were following. They were, but still at the distance they had maintained all morning. Conan was not sure if Bombatta simply wanted to avoid his dust, or if the other warrior simply did not want to ride with him. He suspected the latter, and did not care save for missing the opportunities to look at Jehnna.

As they rode, Malak continually glanced at him

and muttered to himself. After a time he said, "Uh, Conan? What was all that about reasons why I shouldn't be here, and Taramis telling you everything?"

"I wondered when you would ask," Conan grinned, and detailed all that Taramis had said to him. At least, all that related to the seeking of the key and the treasure. Some things, said in his arms, the big youth would definitely not relate.

When he was done Malak shook his head dazedly. "And I thought all I had to worry about was this bringing Valeria back to life. Aiiee! Listen to me! All, I say, as if it was done by every street corner fakir in Shadizar. That's what comes of being too close to too much sorcery, Cimmerian. You're beginning taking it for granted. That is when it will kill you, or worse. Mark my words." He mumbled something quickly, and Conan recognized a prayer to Bel, the Shemitish god of thieves.

"It is not so bad as it could be," the Cimmerian said.

"Not so bad!" Malak all but squealed. "A girl with a map in her head. There is sorcery there, grant me? A magical key guarded by a wizard, and a sorcerous treasure no doubt under the protection of another mage, if not two or three. This is more than a prudent man should expose himself to. Listen. I know three sisters in Arenjun. Triplets, with bodies to make a man weep and a father who's deaf. I'll even let you have two of them. We put Shadizar from our minds, as if we have never been there, or even heard of it. Taramis would never find us in Arenjun, even if she thought to look. Nor would Amphrates. What do you think? We ride for Arenjun, right?''

"And Valeria?" Conan said quietly. "Do I put her from my mind also? Go to Arenjun, if you wish, Malak. I have been there, and have no reason to return.''

"You mean to go on, then?" Malak said. "No matter what I do?" Conan nodded grimly. The smaller man closed his eyes and murmured another prayer, this time to Kyala, the Iranistani goddess of luck. "Very well," he said at last. "I will go with you, Cimmerian. But only because you're giving me your half of Amphrates' gems. This is business.''

"Of course it is," Conan said lightly. "I would never accuse you of doing anything out of friendship.''

"Of course not," Malak said, then frowned suspiciously at the Cimmerian as if he suspected he had not gotten the straight of the exchange. "At least there is one good thing about all of this.''

"What is that?" Conan asked.

"Why, as we are the best thieves in Shadizar," Malak laughed, "which is to say the best in the world, this Amon-Rama will not know we have entered his domain until long after we are gone.''

VI

Once the mountain had brought forth molten rock from the bowels of the earth. A millenium ago had come its final eruption, shaking the ground like the sea in storm for a thousand leagues in all directions, toppling cities and thrones and dynasties. It had blackened the skies with its ash, and in a final, deadly joke, the mountain of fire brought snows where the green of spring should have been and ice in place of the heat of summer for three years. The villagers of the Karpash Mountains no longer remembered why, but they knew it for a mountain of death, and knew their souls were forfeit should they set foot on it.

Half of the mountain had gone in that last, titanic explosion, leaving a long oblong crater with a deep lake, nearly half a league across, at its bottom. Two sides of the great pit were sheer walls, towering a hundred times the height of a man. The other two were gentler slopes, and at the foot of one, abutting the lake, sat a palace such as only one pair of human eyes had ever seen.

Like a gigantic, infinitely faceted gem, the palace was, with towers and turrets and domes of adamantine crystal. No join of stonework showed at any place in it. It seemed a monstrous carving from a single montainous diamond, glittering in the sun.

In the center of that jewel palace was a huge domed chamber, its mirrored walls hidden behind long golden draperies. In the center of the room stood a narrow, pellucid plinth supporting a gem redder than red, a stone glowing as if fire and heart's blood had been compressed and solidified to form it.

Amon-Rama, once a thaumaturge of the Black Ring of Stygia, moved closer to the thin spire, his scarlet hooded robes flowing liquidly about his tall, lean form. His swarthy, narrow face was that of a predator; his nose had the raptor's hook. Ten thousand soulless sorceries had extinguished the last light in his black eyes. Like claws his hands curled about the gem, but he was careful not to touch it. The Heart of Ahriman. Every time his eyes fell on it he exulted.

It was when his former compatriots discovered his possession of the Heart that they expelled him from the Black Circle. Some things even those

dark mages feared to know. Some hidden powers
they dared not risk unveiling. His thin lip curled
contemptuously. He feared nothing, dared anything.
Merely by gaining the gem he had gone beyond
the fools. They would have slain him, had they
managed to find the courage, but each one of them
knew his powers, now that the Heart was his, and
feared the counter-stroke should their attempt fail.

On either side of the Heart his long fingers set
themselves in a precise fashion, and he began to
chant in a language dead for a thousand years.
''A'bath taa'bak, udamai mor'aas. A'bath taa'bak,
endal cafa'ar. A'bath taa'bak, A'bath mor'aas,
A'bath cafa'ar.''

The crystal walls of the palace chimed faintly
with the words, and with each word the glow of
the Heart of Ahriman deepened, deepened and
clarified. Still more crimson than rubies and blood,
it yet became clear as water, and within its depths
figures moved across stony hills.

Amon-Rama's eyes narrowed as he studied the
shapes. Riders. One girl and three men, with two
extra horses. The pattern formed by his fingers
changed slightly, and the girl seemed suddenly to
fill the gem.

The girl, he thought, and smiled cruelly. She
was the One, the One he had sought these many
years. She was attuned to the Heart of Ahriman,
and the Heart to her. The woman in Shadizar
thought to use her. This Taramis had courage, that
she dared think of using the Heart for its ultimate

purpose, and she possessed no small ability in the use of powers, yet she reckoned without Amon-Rama. There were many powers of the stone, many uses other than that one she intended. Once the girl, the One, was in his grasp, he would have access to all of those powers. And he would know which to use, and which not to. He would let this foolish Taramis live, he thought, as a naked bond-maid cowering at his feet. But that was for later.

"Come to me, girl," he whispered. "Bring her to me, my brave warriors. Bring the One to me."

Yet again his fingers formed a new shape about the stone, and he chanted, this time in words never meant to be uttered by a human throat, never meant to be heard by a human ear. They burned in the air like purest pain, and the crystal walls groaned with the agony of them. The Heart of Ahriman glowed redder, brighter, ever brighter. The fierce sanguine light split and coalesced and split again, casting his bloody shadow on every surface of the room till it seemed as if a score of men were there, fifty men, a hundred. And still he chanted, and brighter still grew the piercing light.

A sense of urgency built in Conan, intensifying with his horse's every stride toward the towering Karpash range, so near, now. So near. He must turn aside to find Akiro, he told himself, but the rejoinder came that time was desperately short. Every hour spent seeking the rotund wizard was an hour less available to search out the key, somewhere in the mountains ahead, an hour less to find the treasure and return to Shadizar. Each hour's delay was the risk of being an hour late, the risk that Valeria would not be reborn. The necessity of finding Akiro faded gradually to insignificance; the need to reach the mountains became paramount. Above all else, he must take Jehnna to the mountains.

"Here, Conan."

The Cimmerian turned his head at Malak's words, but he did not slow his mount.

"Akiro," Malak said. He gestured with the hand holding the lead rope of the spare horse. "We must turn south here. That is, we were going to . . . I thought we. . . ." With a shaky laugh, he shook his head. "Maybe it isn't important after all."

Doubtfully Conan reined in. Frowning, he gazed toward the mountains, then to the south, then once more to the mountains. Akiro *was* important; speed was of the essence, delay intolerable.

Bombatta and Jehnna drew their horses up beside the two mis-matched thieves. Strands of the girl's raven hair stuck to her flushed face, and her gaze was fixed on the gray heights filling the horizon.

The black-armored warrior scowled through his sweat. "Why have you stopped, barbar?"

Conan's jaw tightened, but he made no answer. Irritably he twitched the halter rope of the pack mule. Time, he thought. Time. He knew that he wasted time sitting his horse there, neither seeking out the old mage nor riding for the mountains. But which was the correct decision?

"Erlik curse you, barbar, we must keep moving. We are almost to the mountains. We must reach the Heart—the key, we must reach the key quickly!"

Malak broke in on Bombatta's tirade. "What about Akiro, Cimmerian? Do we find him, or not? By Ogun's Toenails, I no longer know *what* to do."

A strangled curse erupted from the scarred man's throat. "Another, barbar? You would add still another to our number? Taramis may say you are essential, but I say you endanger us all! One more in our party may be enough to rupture the prophecy! Or do you care for that at all? Do you just seek delay, fearing to face what lies before us? Do you, you stinking, northland coward?" He ended on a shout, with a handbreadth of sword bared and bloodlust eager on his face.

Conan stared back with glacial eyes. Rage, beyond his strength to control, burst into white heat. His words were flat and hard. "Draw your sword, Zamoran. Draw it and die. I can take Jehnna to the key just as easily without you."

Abruptly Jehnna rode her horse between the two glaring men. To the surprise of both, her large brown eyes snapped with fire. "Cease this, both of you!" she commanded sharply. "You are to escort me to the key. How can you do that if you squabble like two dogs in an alley?"

Conan blinked in disbelief. Had a mouse attacked a cat he could not have been more taken aback.

Bombatta's jaw had dropped open as she spoke. Now he snapped it shut, but he sheathed his steel as well. "We go to the mountains," he told her gruffly.

Ruthlessly Conan quenched the anger that threatened to flare again, controlled his emotions as tightly as the leather wrappings of his swordhilt. Outwardly calm, he turned his horse south.

"You cannot!" Jehnna protested. A small fist pounded on the pommel of her saddle in frustration. The imperious air was gone like gossamer on the wind. "Conan! You are supposed to go the way I show you. You are *supposed* to!"

With a sigh the big Cimmerian stopped and looked back over his shoulder. "Jehnna, this is no game played in the gardens of your aunt's palace. I do what I must, not what anyone thinks I am supposed to do."

"I think it's very much like a game," Jehnna said sulkily. "Like a giant maze, only now you refuse to play."

"In this maze," Conan told her, "death may lie around any turning."

"Of course not!" The slender girl's face was a portrait of shock. "My aunt has raised me for this. It is my destiny. She would not have sent me if I might be harmed."

Conan stared. "Of course not," he said slowly.

"Jehnna, I will take you to the key, and the treasure, and back to Shadizar, and I promise I will allow no harm to come to you. But you must come with me, now, for we may well need the abilities of the man I seek."

Hesitantly, Jehnna nodded. "Very well. I will come with you."

Once more Conan started south, and Malak and Jehnna rode close behind. Scarred face as dark as a thunderhead, Bombatta followed at a distance.

There were no shadows in the chamber of mirrors within the crystal palace. The vermilion blaze was gone, and the Heart of Ahriman gave off only its normal sanguine glow.

Amon-Rama staggered slightly as he walked away from the crystalline plinth that supported the gem. His narrow face seemed narrower still, and pale beneath its swarthiness. There was effort involved in working sorceries at a distance. He needed rest and sustenance before he could try again.

For the moment, however, he thought less of food or sleep than of the failure of his enchantment. He had been unable to see what occurred on the plain; the Heart could not be used to scry and as a nexus of power at one and the same time. He rejected out of hand the possibility that the girl had had anything to do with it. She was the One, true, but no wielder of thaumaturgies. Her life had but one purpose, and sorcery was forbidden to her by the very nature of what was required of her.

That left only the men with her. They were not mages either. He would have detected vibrations of their power when first he viewed them in the Heart, had that been so. Any talisman capable of shielding them from the energies he had unleashed would have showed as clearly as a wizard. That left only a single answer, however impossible it seemed. One of them—one of the two warriors, surely—possessed a force of will so strong as to pass belief.

The Stygian necromancer's smile was cruel. An adamantine will. Beyond acquisition of the girl, there might be sport to be had from such a one.

But first, food and wine and sleep. Wearily Amon-Rama left the chamber of mirrors. On its thin, transparent column the Heart of Ahriman smouldered malevolently.

VII

The sanguinary sun sat on the mountain tops, a burning ball that baked the four riders even as daylight dwindled. Bombatta had cursed steadily since they turned south, but he did it under his breath, and Conan did not try to hear what was said. Had he heard, he might have had to take action, and he had decided that Jehnna should not have to see the other man slain, pleasant though the idea might seem were she not there.

"Over this next hill, Conan," Malak said suddenly. "Selket stab me if Akiro's camp does not lie there. If I was not lied to in Shadizar."

"Three times have you said that," Jehnna said irritably.

The wiry man shrugged and grinned. "Even I make mistakes now and again, my lady. But this time, I assure you, I am right."

Stones turned beneath the hooves of Conan's mount as it made its way up the slope. The Cimmerian was beginning to wonder if Malak even had an idea in which country Akiro was to be found. Then he topped the hill, and growled, "Hannuman's Stones!"

"Watch your tongue before Jehnna!" Bombatta snarled, but as he reached Conan's side he muttered, "Black Erlik's Bowels and Bladder!"

Below them was indeed Akiro's camp, a crude hut of clay and stone built into the side of a hill. The plump, yellow-skinned wizard, however, was bound hand and foot to a thick, upright post set in the ground before the hut, and about his feet piled branches were just leaping into flame. Three men, their backs to those on the hill, stood in front of the growing fire with heads thrown back to chant at the sky and arms outstretched so that their long, white robes hung beneath them like wings. More than a score of others, their filthy, tattered rags contrasting sharply with the triad's pristine garments, watched, howling and shaking their spears in approbation.

"I never liked Akiro all that much," Malak said weakly.

"We need him," Conan replied. He looked at Bombatta, not asking the question, but the Zamoran saw it in his eyes.

"No, barbar. If this is the man you've brought us all this way to find, then he is your affair."

"Why are you all talking," Jehnna demanded

angrily, "instead of helping that poor man down there? Bombatta?"

"My duty is to guard you, child. Would you have me take you among those savages below, or leave you here alone when there might be others about?"

"There is still time to ride for Arenjun," Malak suggested.

"Go straight for Akiro, Malak." Conan's broadsword came easily into his hand, the setting sun lighting its length with premonitory crimson. "He cannot stand those flames much longer." With that he kicked his horse into a gallop down the hill.

"Donar help me," Malak hissed at the Cimmerian's back, "think you of the kind of men who can tie up a wizard!" Muttering quick prayers to half a score of gods, the small thief loosed the horse he had brought for Akiro and followed.

Silently Conan charged, the clash of shod hooves on stone drowned beneath the yells and chants of the spearmen before him. His horse burst into a knot of them, throwing suddenly screaming men to either side like a ship breasting a wave. Others scrambled toward him, spears dropping to the ready, but he ignored them for the moment. The white-clad trio had not ceased their chanting, nor looked away from Akiro. Wizardry of some kind it surely was, and the Cimmerian was just as sure it must be halted if Akiro was to be saved.

The center of the three went down beneath the

hooves of Conan's horse with a startled scream and the crunch of bone. The big youth had no compunction about riding him down from behind. This was no sport, but rather war in miniature. These men meant to kill a friend of his, and he would stop them how he could.

The long-robed man to his right snarled at him, produced a dagger from his voluminous sleeve. The Cimmerian could not help staring in horror even as his sword went up. That snarling mouth held teeth filed to points, and below it hung a necklace of shriveled human hands. Small hands. Children's hands.

Conan made his first sound then since leaving the hilltop, a roar of rage as his steel slashed into that foul, sharp-toothed gap. With a gurgling scream the man jerked himself off the blade. Clawed hands rose to clutch at a ruined face; blood poured between quivering fingers, and spreading scarlet stained the pale robe.

Then Conan had no more time to think of the wizard, if such he was, or of the last of the three, who seemed to have disappeared. Shock had frozen the trio's followers at first. Now they came at a rush.

The first spear to thrust at him Conan grabbed just behind the head, ripping it from the grasp of a man whose throat was torn out by the Cimmerian's broadsword an instant later. With the haft of that spear he beat aside another thrust while his blade was slicing yet another shaft in two. Desperately he shifted his hold on the spear and sank its long point into the face of one of his attackers. His steel clove a skull to the eyes.

Three were dead in as many heartbeats, and the rest fell back. They were enough to sweep over him by sheer weight of numbers, but some would surely die. They had proof of that, now, and none wanted to be in the forefront. They shuffled nervously, edging forward, darks eyes burning with a mixture of fear and shame at that fear.

Carefully, not taking his eyes from the slowly approaching spearmen, Conan stepped down from his horse. They would have the advantage, with their long spears, should he remain mounted. Not, he told himself wryly, that there was not some advantage for them merely in outnumbering him twenty to one. Best to take the initiative. He eyed their straggly line, chose the weakest point, and set himself to attack.

Suddenly a ball of fire shot past his shoulder to strike a ragged spearman in the face and explode in lumps of charred flesh.

Conan jumped in spite of himself, and looked over his shoulder. Beside the fire Malak capered wildly, grinning like a fool. In front of the wiry little thief stood Akiro, his rough brown tunic and cross-gaitered leggings still smouldering in patches. The old wizard's lips moved as if he were chanting, but no sound emerged that Conan could hear. Parchment-skinned hands moved in elaborate patterns, ending in a clap at chest height. And when

Akiro's hands parted another fireball hurtled from between his palms. Immediately he began gesturing again, but two corpses with blackened stumps where their heads had been were more than enough. Howling with terror the rag-clad spearmen threw down their weapons and ran into the deepening twilight. Their cries faded quickly to the south.

"Misbegotten, half-breed spawn of diseased camels!" Akiro muttered. He peered at his hands, blew on his palms, dusted them together. His wispy gray hair and long mustaches stood out in disarrayed spikes. He smoothed them angrily. "I will teach them a lesson to make their grandchildren's grandchildren shake at the mention of my name. I will make their blood freeze and their bones quiver like jelly."

"Akiro," Conan said. Malak squatted to listen, an interested expression on his face.

"I will visit them with a plague of boils to the tenth generation. I will make their herds fail, and their manhoods whither, and their teeth fall out!"

"Akiro," Conan said.

The saffron-skinned mage shook a fist in the direction of the fleeing men. "They claimed I maligned their gods. Gods!" He grimaced and spat. "Fool shamans do not know a fire elemental when they see one. I told them if they sacrificed one more child I would bring lightning down on their heads, and by the Nine-Fold Path of Power, I will do it!"

"Maybe you can't," Malak said. "I mean, they

managed to tie you up and half cook you. Maybe you had better leave them alone.''

Akiro's faced smoothed to an utter lack of expression. "Do not fear, Malak," he said mildly. "I will not make your stones fall off." Malak toppled over backwards, staring with bulging eyes at the wizard. "Is that proper respect that I see on your face?" Akiro asked gently. "Then I shall recount what happened. The three shamans, who call themselves priests, managed to put a spell on me while I slept. A minor spell, but it enabled their followers to fall on me and bind me." His tone hardened as he spoke, and his voice rose higher word by word. "They tied my hands, so I could make no gesture of significance. They stuffed rags into my mouth," he paused to spit, "so I could utter no words of power. Then they proposed to sacrifice me to their gods. Gods! I will show them gods! I shall be a demon in their pantheon, at least, before I am done! I—. That girl."

Conan blinked. He had decided to let Akiro run out of wind—it was the only thing to do when the old mage got the bit firmly between his teeth like this—but the sudden softening of voice and change of subject caught him by surprise. Bombatta, he realized, was finally bringing Jehnna down from the hill. The pair of them were barely visible shapes in the dusk, and Conan, for all his mountain-bred vision, would not have wagered that either was a woman had he not known it already.

"She is an innocent," Akiro said, and Malak laughed shrilly.

"You mean that you can tell from here that she's never—"

"Hold your tongue, Malak!" the old man snapped. "This has naught to do with the flesh. It is of the spirit, and it is a terrible thing."

"Terrible!" Conan exclaimed. "It is not what I would chose for myself, but terrible?"

Akiro nodded. "Such must be protected like children till they gain some knowledge of the world, else they are fated to be prey. It is rare that an innocent occurs naturally. Most have been raised so for some sorcerous purpose."

"Raised so," Conan murmured, frowning. Well away from the hut, and the bodies before it, Bombatta was helping Jehnna down from her mount. The black-armored warrior stood between her and the charnel scene, not allowing her to look.

"Valeria," Akiro said, and the Cimmerian started.

"She is part of why I came to you, Akiro."

"Wait." Akiro bustled into the rude hut. Oaths and the clatter of rummaging drifted out. When he returned he handed Conan a small, polished stone vial sealed with beeswax. "This is for Valeria," he said.

"I do not understand," Conan said.

Akiro pursed his lips and tugged at his mustaches, one with either hand. "Long did I study this question, Cimmerian. I tossed the Bones of Fate, read the stars, told the K'far cards, all to find an answer for what troubles you.''

"I am troubled no longer, Akiro. At least—''

"Do not dissemble with me,'' the wizard cut him off. "How can I help if you do not speak truth to me? Valeria's life and yours were most strongly intertwined. She was at once lover and companion warrior. She died in your place, and so strong was the bond between you that even death could not stop her returning to save you. Cimmerian, that great a bond between life and death is dangerous. Valeria would sever it herself if she knew, but some knowledge is hidden to those beyond the dark.''

"Akiro, I do not want the bond severed, and it is not necessary.''

"Listen to me, you stubborn northlander. You cannot cut your way out of this with a sword. I know your fate if you will not listen. The cards, the bones, the stars, all agree. Eventually the bond will pull you into a living death. You will find yourself trapped halfway between the world of the living and the world of the dead, but in neither, able to touch neither, for the rest of time. Only forgetfulness can save you. I went to great pains to concoct the potion in that vial. It will wipe from your mind all memory of Valeria. Naught connected to her will remain. Believe me, Cimmerian, could she know the choice you face, Valeria would tell you to drink from that vial without delay. She was not one to shirk a hard decision.''

"And if Valeria could return once more?" Conan asked quietly. "Not for moments, as she did before, but to live the rest of the life she should have had. What then, Akiro?"

The rotund mage was silent for a long moment. His eyes traveled to Jehnna, and he licked his lips slowly. "I think we must clear away these bodies so we can eat," he said finally. "I shall need food in me to hear this."

VIII

The old wizard would not take back his vial, and finally Conan stuffed it into his belt pouch. In the end it was he and Malak who dragged the corpses away. Akiro muttered vaguely about his back and his aged bones, though there was considerable muscle under those layers of fat. Bombatta again refused to leave Jehnna, or to let her come close enough to see what the big Cimmerian and his diminutive friend carried to the far side of the hill.

Akiro had said he required food before listening, and now he insisted on it. Rabbits taken that morning by the wizard—by the normal means of a sling and stone—were spitted and roasted, and a half-filled basket of small Corinthian oranges was produced from the hut. Finally the last bones were gnawed, and orange peels were tossed into the fire that cast a golden pool before the small hut. Bombatta took a wetstone from his pouch and bent himself to tending his tulwar's edge. Malak began juggling three of the oranges to the delight of Jehnna, though he dropped one at every second pass.

'' 'Tis a part of the trick,'' the wiry thief said as he picked an orange from the ground for the fourth time. ''To make the later things I do seem even greater by comparison.''

Akiro touched Conan on the arm and motioned with his head to the darkness. The two men withdrew from the fire; none of the others seemed to notice their going.

When they had gone far enough that their voices would not carry back to the hut, Akiro said, ''Now tell me how Valeria is to be brought back to life.''

Conan eyed the plump mage speculatively, though he could see nothing of his visage but shadows in the moonlight. Wizards did things in their own way and for their own reasons, even the most benign of them. Not that many could be called benign. Even Akiro, with whom he had traveled before, was largely a mystery to him. But then, was there *anyone* in all of this whom he could afford to trust totally?

''Taramis,'' Conan began, ''the Princess Royal, has promised to return Valeria to me. Not as a shade, nor as an animated corpse, but living, as once she lived.''

The wizard was silent for a time, tugging at the

long mustaches that framed his mouth. "I would not have thought to find one of such power alive in the world today," he said finally. "Most especially not as a princess of the Zamoran Royal house."

"You think she lies?" Conan sighed, but Akiro shook his head.

"Perhaps not. It is written that Malthaneus of Ophir did this thing a thousand years gone, and possibly Ahmad Al-Rashid, in Samara, twice so far in the past. It could be that it is time for the world to once more see such wonders."

"Then you believe Taramis can do as she promised."

"Of course," Akiro continued musingly, "Malthaneus was the greatest white wizard since the Circle of the Right-Hand Path was broken in the days before Acheron, and Ahmad Al-Rashid, it is said, was thrice-blessed by Mitra himself."

"You jump about like a monkey," Conan growled. "Can you not say one thing or another and stick to it?"

"I can say that this thing has been done in the past. I can say that Taramis *may* be able to do it." He paused, and Conan thought his bushy gray brows had drawn down into a frown. "But why should she do it for you?"

In as few words as possible the Cimmerian told of the quest on which he accompanied Jehnna, of the key and the treasure and the short time that remained.

"A Stygian," Akiro muttered when he had finished. "It is said that there is no people without some spark of good in them, but never have I found a Stygian I would trust long enough to turn around twice."

"He must be a powerful sorcerer," Conan said. "No doubt too powerful for you."

Akiro wheezed a short laugh. "Do not try that game on me, youngling. I am too old to be snared so easily. I have those accursed hedge-wizards to deal with."

"I would not find your company amiss, Akiro."

"I am too old to go riding off into the mountains, Cimmerian. Come, let us go back to the fire. The nights are cold here, and the fire is warm." Rubbing his hands together, the gray-haired mage did not wait for Conan to follow.

"At least Bombatta will be quieted," Conan muttered. "He has been afraid Malak or you would upset some part of the prophecy of Skelos."

Akiro froze with one foot lifted for his next step. Slowly he turned back to face the big youth. "Skelos?"

"Aye, the Scrolls of Skelos. They tell what is to be found on this quest, and what must be done for it to succeed, or so says Taramis. You know of this Skelos?"

"A thaumaturge centuries dead," Akiro replied absently, "who wrote many volumes of sorcerous lore. All now as rare as virgins in Shadizar." He thrust his head forward, staring intently at Conan through the darkness. "Taramis has these in her possession? The Scrolls of Skelos?"

"She quoted from them as if she does. She must. Where are you going?"

Akiro was disappearing toward the hut with a quickness that belied his complaints of feebleness. "Time is short, you say," he called over his shoulder. "We must leave for the mountains before first light, and I need my sleep."

Smiling, Conan strolled after him. Betimes, he thought, the best snare was one you did not know you had laid.

When the Cimmerian reached the fire Jehnna sat staring into the flames with daydreaming eyes. Bombatta, still drawing the wetstone along his blade, shot irritable glances at Malak, who sprawled beneath a blanket with snores like ripping sailcloth coming from his open mouth. The scar-faced warrior was not the only one bothered by the all-intrusive sound. From within the hut came angry mutters, of which only the words ". . . need my sleep," ". . . old bones," and ". . . like an ox with a bad belly," were recognizable.

Abruptly Akiro's frowning face appeared in the doorway of the hut, eyes fixed intently on Malak and lips moving. Malak's snore ended as if sliced by a razor. With a gasp the wiry thief bolted upright, staring about him fearfully. Akiro was no longer to be seen. Hesitantly, one hand feeling at his throat, Malak stretched himself out again. His breathing deepened quickly, but barely enough to be heard above the crackle of the fire. Moments later snorting rumbles began to erupt from the hut.

Jehnna giggled. "Is he going with us?"

"Yes." Conan sat crosslegged beside her. "We will leave before the sun rises."

"In the direction I say, this time?"

"In the direction you say."

He could feel her eyes on him; they made him unaccustomedly awkward. He had no small experience with women. He could deal with impudent serving girls and old merchants' too-young wives, with brazen doxies and nobles' hot-eyed daughters. This girl was a virgin and more. An innocent, Akiro termed her, and Conan thought the word fit. Still, there was one thing that did *not* fit with that description.

"Before," Conan said, "when Bombatta and I all but came to blows, you changed, for a space of moments at least. You sounded much like Taramis."

"For a few moments I *was* Taramis." His eyes widened, and she giggled. "Oh, not in truth. I did not want the two of you fight, so I pretended that I was my aunt, and that two of the servants were squabbling."

"I am no servant," Conan said sharply.

Jehnna seemed taken aback. "Why do you sound offended? You serve my aunt, and me. Bombatta is not offended that he is my aunt's servant."

The sussuration of wetstone on steel stopped, unnoticed by the two at the fire.

"He can bend his knee if he wishes," Conan

said. "I hire my sword and my skill for a day, or for ten, but I am servant to no man, woman or god."

"All the same," she replied, "I am glad that you accompany me. I cannot remember ever speaking more than two words together to anyone other than my aunt, or Bombatta, or my dressing maids. You are very different, and interesting. It is all different and interesting. The sky and the stars and so many leagues and leagues of open space."

He stared into her big brown eyes and felt a hundred years older than she. As lovely a maiden as he had ever seen, he thought, and so very truly the innocent indeed, unknowing of the feelings she could raise in a man. "It is a dangerous land," he muttered, "and the mountains are more so, even without a Stygian sorcerer. This is no place for you."

"It is my destiny," she said simply, and he grunted.

"Why? Because it is written in the Scrolls of Skelos?"

"Because I was marked at birth. Look."

Before his astonished eyes Jehnna tugged down the neck of her robes, shrugging, until her satiny olive-skinned breasts were bared almost to the nipples. Sweet mounds made to nestle in a man's palms, the Cimmerian thought, his throat suddenly tight.

"See?" Jehnna said. "Here. This mark I bore

at birth, naming my destiny. It is described in the scrolls, but it was the gods who chose me.''

There was a birthmark, he saw, in the valley between her breasts. A red eight-pointed star, no bigger than a man's thumbnail and as precisely formed as if drawn by a craftsman.

Abruptly curved steel slashed down to shine in the firelight between them.

''Do not touch her, thief,'' Bombatta grated. ''Not ever!''

Conan opened his mouth for an angry reply, then realized that he had indeed been stretching a hand toward the girl. The gleaming blade hung before his fingertips as if it was the tulwar he had meant to stroke. Furious with himself, Cimmerian straightened, returning Bombatta's glare.

Jehnna's eyes traveled from one man to the other, a strange expression crossing her face as if thoughts new and disturbing had come to her.

''It is late,'' Conan said harshly. ''Best we all sleep, for we must travel early.''

Bombatta held out his free hand to help Jehnna rise, still holding his blade before her as if it were a shield. Conan's eyes did not leave those of the scarred warrior while the huge Zamoran backed away, leading Jehnna. The girl glanced once at the tall Cimmerian youth, her eyes troubled, but she allowed herself to be bundled into her blankets without speaking. As on the previous night Bombatta set himself before her as a guard.

Muttering curses under his breath, Conan wrapped

himself in his own blankets. This was foolishness, he told himself. There were women enough in the world that he did not let himself be entangled by a girl who likely did not even know what she did. She was a child, no matter her age. He slept, and his sleep was filled with dreams of lush-bodied Taramis and the night of lust they had shared. Yet often, in those dreams, he would look, and it would be not Taramis he held, but Jehnna. His sleep was not a restful one.

Blackness hung thickly over Shadizar, and the tapestried halls of Taramis' palace were empty as she made her way from her sleeping chamber. The only sound was the brushing of her long silken robe on the polished marble tiles of the corridors. Her astrologers and the priests of the ancient worship she revived came often to the great hall she entered, but the nocturnal visits that she made with increasing frequency, she made alone.

About the edges of the room cunningly hooded golden lamps gave off a soft glow that could have been moonlight, so pale was it. The floor was black marble, polished to a mirror sheen, and fluted alabaster columns supported the high, arched ceiling, tiled with onyx and set with sapphires and diamonds to represent the night sky, the sky as it would be on one night in each thousand years.

Centered beneath that false sky was a couch carved of crimson marble, polished with the hair of virgins, and on it lay what seemed to be the alabaster statue of a man with his eyes closed, nude and half again as large as any living man, more handsome than any mortal man could ever be. But a single thing marred the perfection. Sunk to the depth of half a finger joint in the broad forehead was a black depression, a circle as wide as man's hand. There was about the figure a sense of timeless waiting.

Slowly Taramis approached the marble couch, stopping at its foot. Her gaze roamed the alabaster form, and her breath quickened. Many men had she had in her life, choosing the first most carefully at sixteen, choosing each since with as great a care. Men she knew as well as she knew the rooms of her own palace. But what would it be like to be the lover of . . . a god?

She slipped her robe from her shoulders and sank naked to her knees at the feet of the figure. No word in the Scrolls of Skelos required this of her, but she wanted more than even they promised.

Pressing her face to those cold, alabaster soles she whispered, "I am thine, O great Dagoth."

A compulsion to go further than ever before seized her, and she rained moaning kisses on those feet. Slowly she worked her way upwards, leaving no portion of that pale surface undampened by her ardent lips, caressing it with her lush roundness, until she writhed atop the great form as she would atop a man. Trembling fingers reached up to softly stroke the face.

"I am thine, O great Dagoth," she whispered

again, "and forever will I be thine. When thou wakeneth I will build temples to thee, overturning the temples of other gods, but I will be more than thy priestess. Thy godly flesh will merge with mine, and I will hold myself chaste hereafter, save for thee. I will sit on thy right hand, and by thy grace will I receive the ultimate powers over life and death. Once more will the sacrifices be made to thee, and once more to thee will the nations bow. All this I vow, O great Dagoth, and seal it with my flesh and my soul."

Suddenly her breath caught in her throat. That on which she lay had still the hardness of stone, but now it held the warmth of life. Not daring to believe, fearing that perhaps it was but the heat of her own body, absorbed, she brought her hands down over the broad, perfect shoulders to the deep chest. Everywhere was the warmth.

Almost at once it was gone again, and her last doubts were shattered by the unnatural quickness of its going. Her god had given her a sign. Her offering would be accepted; the rewards would be hers. Smiling, she let her own sleep claim her there, lying atop the form of the Sleeping God.

ix

Conan's eyes narrowed as he studied what lay ahead. Shadows stretched before him, and behind the sun had not yet risen two handbreadths above the horizon. There were shadows in plenty on the sheer rock wall that faced them half a league on, the narrow lines of folds and creases in the stone, but no sign of any pass.

"Jehnna?" he called, looking over his shoulder.

He did not have to say more. All had fallen silent as they saw what they approached, and even the slender girl wore a worried frown.

"We must go this way," she said insistently. "I know this is the right way. Straight ahead now. I know it."

Conan booted his horse into a trot. Whatever lay ahead—and there had better be *something*, by all the gods—he was impatient to find out what it was.

He scanned the cliffs, running a league to the north and south of the point they rode toward. The lowest was at least fifty paces in height and topped with a jutting overhang, the highest was ten times that. Occasional vertical crevices and shadowed chimneys split the continuous front, but in those two leagues was nothing that even hinted at a passage through.

He could climb it, he knew. He had climbed higher cliffs and sheerer in the wind-swept mountain fastnesses of his native Cimmeria. Malak likely could, as well, and perhaps even Bombatta, but Akiro was no scaler of cliffs, and the Cimmerian could see no way at all to get Jehnna over them unless she grew wings. Wings. He hummed thoughtfully. Actual wings were out of the question, of course, but perhaps Akiro could provide an answer. Mayhap the old man could use his powers to lift himself and the girl to the top of the cliff while the rest of them climbed in more ordinary fashion.

Abruptly he realized what lay directly ahead of him. Straight ahead, she had said, and straight ahead was a narrow crevice, but a crevice that stretched deep into the cliff, losing his eyes with a sharp bend in fifty paces. He could not be so lucky, he was sure, that this would not be their path. Wings, he thought, would have been much better.

Conan looked around at the others. It was clear by their faces that they all saw what he had seen. Even Bombatta wore a doubtful grimace, and Malak was muttering prayers under his breath. Only Jehnna appeared sure, and even so the Cimmerian could not help asking.

"This?" She nodded firmly, and he sighed. "I will go first," he said, loosening his broadsword in its worn leather scabbard. "Malak behind me, then Akiro and the packhorse, then Jehnna. Bombatta, you bring up the rear." The scar-faced warrior nodded, easing his own curved blade. "And keep a watch above," he finished. Though, he thought, what they could do if someone began dropping boulders or worse on them he could not imagine.

"Shakuru's Burning Teeth," Malak said sourly. "We could have been in Arenjun by now."

Not answering, Conan rode into the narrow opening, and the rest followed. The sky became a thin strip directly overhead, and light faded till it almost seemed twilight was upon them once more. The high walls were barely separated enough to allow horse and rider to pass. Gray stone slid past, often no more than a fingerwidth from knees on either side.

On they rode, twisting, turning, doubling back on themselves, till only Conan's instincts told him that they still moved westward. The sun stood directly overhead, now, throwing a cascade of fading shadows into the snaking gap.

Suddenly Conan drew rein, his nostrils flaring.

"What is it?" Bombatta called hoarsely.

"Have you no nose?" the Cimmerian demanded.

"Woodsmoke," Akiro said.

"Aye," Conan agreed. "And more than a campfire."

"What do we do?" Malak wanted to know, and Conan snorted with brief laughter.

"What can we do, my friend? We ride on and see what's burned."

Three more bends the strait passage took, and then they were out of it. Out of the narrow crack through the mountain, and into a large village that butted against the steep side of the valley. Crude huts lined dusty paths that could not properly be called streets. On the far side of the village Conan noted half-a-score wispy columns of smoke, remnants of whatever had burned. A few naked children yelled and tumbled in the dirt with bony dogs, while their ragged elders, as filthy as the small ones if not more so, stared in dark-eyed surprise and wariness at the newcomers.

"Pull up the hood of your cloak, Jehnna," the Cimmerian said quietly.

"It is hot," she protested, but Bombatta jerked the white hood forward, hiding her face in its shade.

Conan nodded. As outlanders they might well have trouble just riding through this village, and most assuredly there was no way around it. There was no need to increase the chance by letting it be known they included a beautiful young girl in their number.

"Do not stop for anything," he told the others, "until we are well beyond this place. Not for anything." Resting a hand on his swordhilt, he twitched his reins and started forward. They rode in the same order in which they had traveled the narrow passage.

"Malak," Akiro said, "if you see something you desire in this place, try not to steal it."

"Eh?" Malak jerked his hand back from a basket of figs. "Fidesa's Teats, old man, I am not a fool."

Suspicious eyes followed them, covetous eyes that caressed their horses and weapons, speculative eyes that tried to pierce Jehnna's cloak. Yet they were not many for such a place, and as they came on the source of the smoke, ten patches of ash that had once been huts, Conan saw why there were not more. The villagers had gathered to watch a brutal entertainment.

Six soldiers in boiled leather breastplates and red-crested helms stood leaning on their spears and laughing in a wide circle around a woman who clutched a wooden staff taller than she and as thick as a man's two thumbs. Her skin, as black as polished ebony, proclaimed her origin far to the south. A tightly bound strip of cloth about her small breasts and a slightly wider bit about her loins were all of the garb on her hard-muscled body, and a thick rope bound about one ankle kept her within a pace of a stake driven into the ground.

"Those men are not Zamorans," Jehnna said. "This is Zamoran land, is it not?"

Conan did not think that it was the proper moment to explain the border situation to her. The men wore the armor of one of the Corinthian city-states. The mountains, on the border between Zamora and Corinthia, were claimed by both, and the villages paid such taxes as they could not avoid to whomever sent soldiers, denying the sovereignty of either when there were no soldiers.

The black woman stooped slowly, not taking her eyes from the encircling soldiers, to feel the knot at her ankle. As her fingers touched the rope, one of the Corinthians dashed forward, jabbing with his spear. The woman leaped back as far as the rope would allow, the staff spinning in her hands like a thing alive. The spearman stopped his rush, laughing, and another, behind her, jumped forward. Again she darted away from the spearpoint, then had to dodge yet another.

"What did this woman do to deserve this?" Jehnna demanded. Conan stifled an oath, and gripped his sword hilt more firmly.

A dirty-faced man on the edge of the crowd looked up at Jehnna, frowning. "She's a bandit." He twisted his neck, trying to see her face under the edge of her hood. "We took another, and killed him slow, but the soldiers came before we could get to her."

"They'll do for her," another man said, joining the attempt to make out Jehnna's features. A swollen bruise stood out blue beneath the grime on his forehead. "They shouldn't have given that stick back, though. She killed a man with it, and near got away." His gaze slid from Jehnna to each of the others in turn, and his mouth pursed thoughtfully.

"Bombatta," Jehnna said, "you must stop them. Whatever she has done, these men have no right to treat her so. They are Corinthians, and this is Zamoran land."

"Bandits and thieves deserve to die," the scar-faced Zamoran said harshly. "And it is time we were going on." He snatched for her bridle, missing as she pulled her horse around to face Conan.

"And will you do nothing either?" she demanded.

Conan drew a deep breath, but the situation had gone beyond cursing. More villagers were turning to look at them, weighing the value of their possessions with intent eyes, trying to see if Jehnna were pretty enough for the auction block. Such were not usually dangerous in the open and the daylight, but their blood was heated by the bandits' raid, and by the soldiers' cruel sport. The desire was there, writ plain on their faces in licked lips and shifting glances. In moments, soldiers or no, daylight or no, these men would try for fresh prey, and an attempt to leave now would only set off the eruption on the instant.

"Stand ready," the Cimmerian commanded quietly.

"Bel watch over us," Malak breathed as Conan moved his horse into the crowd.

Wondering villagers parted slowly before him as he rode slowly toward the soldiers. Casually, nodding to the Corinthians, he rode into their circle. They frowned at each other, at him, obviously unsure what he was about. He drew his broadsword.

"Do not kill her and spoil the fun!" one of the Corinthians shouted. The sable-skinned woman stepped smoothly to the limits of the rope, her staff at the ready and untrusting eyes on his face.

Conan gave her a smile he hoped was reassuring. His blade flashed in the sun, slashing through the rope close to her ankle. Their eyes met; she had not moved a muscle. There was no fear in her, he thought admiringly.

"What did he do?" a soldier called. "I could not see. Did he strike her?"

As casually as he had entered the circle, Conan rode out of it, heedless of the doubtful glances the Corinthians cast at him. Before the Cimmerian reached his companions the black woman took advantage of her chance. Staff moaning with the speed of its whirling, she attacked.

"Ride!" Conan roared.

The thick butt of the woman's weapon crushed a soldier's throat before her captors had time to realize she was truly free of the rope. The wooden shaft crashed against a crested helmet, buckling the Corinthian's knees, then spun to shiver a spear from another's grasp and rebound into his face with the crunch of bone and a spray of blood.

Shouting villagers scattered before Conan's waving sword and prancing horse. Bombatta struggled to reach Jehnna's reins, while she protested, yelling words the Cimmerian could not hear and pointing at the woman who fought.

Three soldiers had gone down in almost the space of as many breaths, and the three remaining hesitated at closing with the woman responsible. She whirled the long staff about her head, giving a high, ululating cry. The three exchanged glances and reached their decision. As one man, they ran. Again the woman gave voice to her battle cry, this time in triumph. Then she disappeared after the soldiers.

Angrily Conan snatched Jehnna's reins from her hands. She tried to speak, but he booted his horse to a gallop, pulling hers behind, and all she could do was cling to the high pommel of her saddle. Villagers shook fists at them, and here or there a spear or rusty sword, but they made no effort to hinder the speeding riders.

Only when the village was out of sight around a bend in the valley did Conan slow, and return the girl's reins to her.

She snatched them from his hand and glared. "Why did we leave that woman in the village? She—"

"She has more chance now than she did an hour

gone," Conan barked. "Did we come here to rescue bandits, or to find a key?" He made an effort to control his anger. She had no idea of the danger in which she had placed them, not even now.

A clatter of hooves in the distance brought a growl from Bombatta. "The Corinthians. There's little chance they will leave us out of their report."

"They will leave out the dark-skinned woman," Akiro observed drily, "and make us many more than we are. To be driven off by a large party of armed men is one thing, to be defeated by a single woman another."

Jehnna looked from one to another of them. "We had to do it," she maintained stubbornly. "That woman could not have deserved to be tormented."

"Which way?" Conan asked, breathing heavily.

Jehnna pointed silently down the valley. At least, the Cimmerian thought, it was not back toward the village. There was no talk among them as they resumed their journey.

X

The valley down which they fled from the village led into another valley, that into yet another, and the third into a twisting, steep-walled canyon scattered with huge boulders, some half-buried in the stony soil. The Karpash Mountains loomed about them, gray peaks often capped with snow, their dark lower slopes sparsely spotted with stunted trees.

Conan eyed the sun, halfway to its setting now, and thought of the time left. Only three more days, and they had not even found the key yet, much less the treasure. And if they did not return to Shadizar with both by the night of the third day. . . . Face grim, he touched the golden dragon amulet hanging at his neck.

Malak brought his horse up beside the Cimmerian. "We are being followed, Conan."

Conan nodded. "I know."

"There is only one, but he's getting closer."

"Then we had best dissuade him," Conan said. "You and Akiro keep on with the girl. I will catch up to you." He dropped back until he rode with Bombatta at the rear. "We are being followed," he told the scarred man.

"I know," Bombatta replied.

"Let us convince him not to, you and I."

Bombatta frowned doubtfully at Jehnna before giving a reluctant nod.

As the others continued on their way, the two men swung their horses from the line of march, one to either side. Two of the great boulders that dotted the valley shielded them from whomever came up the trail after them. Jehnna twisted in her saddle to look back, but Conan motioned quickly for her to turn back. The follower must be given no warning that he was discovered. The girl and her two companions disappeared behind another bend of the canyon. Conan drew his sword and rested it across the saddle before him. He did not have long to wait.

Stones rattling beneath shod hooves heralded the approach of their pursuer, and Conan frowned at the noise. The man did not seem to care if he was detected. The Cimmerian exchanged glances with Bombatta, and the two set themselves.

The first glimpse of a horse appeared between the boulders that hid them, and Conan charged out. "Hold!" he shouted, and then his jaw dropped in surprise. Beside him, Bombatta began to curse.

The ebon-skinned woman from the village started and stared, then drew herself up. Her horse, two hands shorter than theirs, bore a Corinthian military saddle, and behind it hung a leather waterbag. "I am Zula," she announced proudly, "a warrior of the People of the Mountain, who live to the south of the land called Keshan. I would know the name of he who gave me my life again."

"I am called Conan," the Cimmerian said, "of Cimmeria."

Zula peered at his face intently. "I did not truly believe your eyes before. Do many people in this Cimmeria have eyes like sapphire?"

"Erlik take his eyes," Bombatta snapped, "and you as well, woman! You have heard his name. Now be on your way, and bother us no more!"

The woman did not look at him, or seem even to have heard him. "I will ride with you, Conan of Cimmeria. Perhaps I can repay the life you gave me."

Conan shook his head slowly. This talk of a life to be repaid was so strong a reminder of Valeria that it must be an omen, but of what kind? "What I did was not done to save your life, but rather to allow us to escape that village without having to fight our way out. You owe me nothing."

"Reasons do not matter," she said. "Only actions. And for your actions I live and am free, where else I would be dead or captive."

Before Conan could frame an answer they were joined by Jehnna and the others.

He gave the two men with her a withering look. "Did I not say I would catch up to you? What if there had been a score of villagers on our trail? Is this how you look after Jehnna?"

Malak grinned weakly and became engrossed in study of the pack horse's lead rope. Akiro shrugged, saying, "I am too old to make a woman do what she does not wish to do."

"Do not be silly, Conan," Jehnna said. "Malak said there was only one, and you agreed. My ears are not failing." She shifted her attention to Zula. "The villagers called you a bandit."

"They lied," the dark woman replied scornfully. "There is a smaller village four leagues to the south, from which these people stole several young women. With other warriors I took payment for the recovery of these women. In the night we came, firing storage huts to draw the attention of these dogs who call themselves men. The women we found, but T'car, who was my battle companion, took a spear thrust and could not escape, and I could not leave him."

"And so you both were captured," Jehnna said breathlessly. "It was a brave thing you did, a thing such as romances are made of."

"He was my battle companion," Zula said simply.

Jehnna jerked a nod, as if reaching a decision. "You will come with us."

"No!" Bombatta shouted. "Mitra's mercies, Jehnna, will you endanger everything? Remember the prophecy."

"I remember nothing that says I cannot have a woman with me." Jehnna's tone was firm, but still she turned to Conan. "Say that she may accompany me. You have Malak and Akiro. I have only Bombatta, and he shouts at me of late. He never shouted at me before."

"She could not even keep up with us on that Corinthian sheep," Malak laughed.

Zula eyed him calmly. "I will ride you into the ground, little man, even after you attain full growth."

Conan touched the amulet on his chest. Bombatta could be right; perhaps they *did* endanger the fulfilling of the prophecy, and thus the rebirth of Valeria. But there was the matter of the omen. A life to be repaid. "I will not say no," he said finally.

Bombatta cursed, but Jehnna overrode him with her enthusiasm. "Then you will ride with me, and be my companion."

"I will ride with Conan," Zula said. "And so with you." Jehnna smiled as if she had not caught the distinction the ebon woman made.

"Let us *all* ride, then," Conan said, and turned his horse once more down the canyon.

In the sanguine glow of the gem Amon-Rama studied the moving figures. Two more, he thought, and concentrated his study on the rotund, yellow-skinned man with the wispy gray hair and mustaches. There was power there. A wizard. His thin mouth twisted in a malevolent smile. Not enough power. Merely more sport.

"Come to me," he whispered. "Bring the One to me."

". . . And when you have carried this key and this treasure to Shadizar," Zula said, "what then?"

Jehnna looked at the other woman in surprise. She had never thought of such a question. "Why, I will live in the palace, as I always have." That brought a vaguely dissatisfied frown to her face. But what else was she to do? "This is my destiny," she said firmly.

Zula only grunted.

Feeling ill at ease without knowing why, Jehnna let her eyes travel ahead, to wiry, laughing Malak and round-bellied, wise-eyed Akiro, to broad-shouldered Conan, riding in the lead as they wended their way around a snow-tipped mountain. Bombatta still brought up the rear, his gaze always on the heights, searching for danger in the fading, reddish-gold light that announced the imminence of dusk.

It was the Cimmerian who held her thoughts, however. He was so different from what she had expected. Akiro, and even Malak, had their places in the stories her dressing maids told, but the tall northlander fit nowhere in those tales of handsome princes and lovely princesses. And it was not just him. He made *her* feel very peculiar, indeed, in ways she did not recognize. None of her feelings seemed to correspond to what she imagined she would feel like if he were to recite long poems to her eyes. It was difficult to imagine him doing that, in any case. Or to see him giving her a single, golden rose for her to weep crystal tears over while he went far away. Conan might rather sweep her fiercely to his saddle before him and . . . and what? She was not sure, but she was certain that whatever he would do would be something not in the stories.

Zula, she thought, might have useful advice, but something made her feel awkward about simply asking. But perhaps if she made her way to it in slow steps. . . .

"Women warriors," she said abruptly, "are strange to me. Are all women of your land warriors?"

The dark woman nodded. "Our mountains are surrounded by enemies, and we are few. Too few to allow us your ways, where only men are warriors, and some few women who want to be. All of us must fight, if we would live."

"I did not know there were women in my land who are warriors," Jehnna said, diverted for the moment. "Could I be a warrior?" It would certainly be a different thing than living the rest of her life in Taramis' gardens, she thought.

"Perhaps," Zula replied, "if you were willing to accept hard training, and if you have the heart.

It is a harsh life, though, and you must ever be ready for death. Your own, or that of someone close to you.''

The sadness in the other woman's voice reminded Jehnna of her purpose. ''T'car,'' she said softly. ''You called him your battle companion. Was he your . . . your true love?''

''My lover, you mean? Aye, he was my lover, and in all ways as good a man as I have ever known.''

''How . . . how did it begin? Between you and T'car, that is.''

Zula laughed, as if at a fond memory. ''Many women wanted him, for he was a proud and handsome man, but I told them they must fight me if they would lie with him. None of them could stand against me, and when T'car saw, he took me into his hut.''

Jehnna blinked. It certainly did not sound like any of the stories. ''So you simply decided he would be yours, chose him. Do men like that?''

''Some men, child, if they know themselves men. Others have not the stomach for it.''

''And which of the men riding with us would you chose? Malak, perhaps?''

The black woman snorted. ''That has no humor even if it is meant to be a joke. I would choose Conan.''

''Because he saved your life?'' Jehnna felt a flash of anger, and could not understand it. ''Why not Bombatta?''

"That one would be brutal, thinking it made him seem strong, yet I could bend him to my will like bending a reed. Conan can be strong and gentle at the same time, and he would not bend easily if at all. As well lie with a rabbit as with a man you can bend too easily." Zula gave her a sidelong glance; Jehnna knew her face was flushed, and the other woman's obvious amusement made her color deepen. "Do not worry, child. I will not try to take him from you."

Jehnna found herself stammering. "Take him . . . but he is not . . . I mean. . . ." She drew a deep breath and tried to sit very straight in her saddle, as Taramis did at her most imperious. "Do not call me child," she said frostily. "I am a woman."

"Of course. Forgive me, Jehnna." Zula was silent for a time before continuing. "Among my people there is a custom at the death of a lover. I will lie with no man for one year from the day of T'car's dying. He would have done the same had I died."

It was Jehnna's turn to ride in silence, mulling over what had been said. Little of it seemed to be of any use to her. There were no women to challenge over Conan, even if she knew how to fight them, and even if she was sure that was what she wanted. As for the rest. . . .

"Zula, thrice now you have spoken of lying with a man. What does that mean?"

The black woman's face went slack with amazement. "By all the gods," she breathed, "you *are* a child."

Jehnna opened her mouth for an angry retort, and froze with it open. Before them lay another mountain, or rather half of a mountain, for its top had long since disappeared. Even from below it was plain that a vast crater holed that truncated peak.

"Conan," she whispered, then shouted it, "Conan! The key! I can feel it pulling me! The key is in that crater!" Eagerly she urged her horse to a gallop.

xi

"Wait, Jehnna," Conan called for the tenth time, but he knew it was already too late. She had outdistanced all of them, and even as he spoke she topped the crater's rim and disappeared.

Cursing, he sped after her as fast as his horse would take the mountain slope. The others were strung out behind him in a long line, but he could not wait for them. Over the rim he galloped, and gasped as he started down the other side.

At the bottom of the mammoth pit lay a lake unruffled by any breeze, its dark blue speaking of great depth. On either side of the glassy waters rose sheer walls. Below him was a small beach of black sand, rushes growing on its edges. Jehnna's mount was already halfway to the water in its headlong plunge. And on the far side of the lake stood a palace of crystal, an impossible structure of glittering facets that made the hair stand up on the back of his neck.

By the time he caught up to her, Jehnna's panting horse had its muzzle in the lake, and the girl stared with eager eyes at the distant crystalline towers. The crater's deepness created an early dusk on the sands.

"The key is in that palace?" Conan said.

She nodded excitedly. "Yes. I can feel it, pulling me."

"We must leave the crater, then," he told her, "and go around the side of the mountain. There is no way from here except to swim."

The others began to arrive, first Bombatta and Zula almost together, then Akiro, and lastly Malak, with the packhorse.

"Are you all right, child?" Bombatta shouted at the same instant that Zula cried, "Jehnna, are you unharmed?" The scar-faced man and the ebon woman glared at one another.

"This is the way," Jehnna said insistently. "This is the proper way."

"How?" Conan demanded.

Even Bombatta looked doubtful. "We could go around, child. It can make no difference."

"This is the way," Jehnna repeated.

Suddenly Malak leaped down from his horse and waded into the rushes. When he came out again he was dragging a long, narrow boat of hides stretched over a wooden frame. He held up a handful of cords and bone fish-hooks. "Villagers provide the way, eh?" he grinned. "The fisherman will not care if we borrow his boat. There are paddles in it, too."

"Convenient," Akiro murmured, "to find it here. Mayhap too convenient."

"What do you mean?" Conan asked.

The wizard tugged at a dangling gray mustache and peered toward the palace, sparkling still even now that direct sunlight was gone. "I do not think the Karpash Mountain folk are fishermen. And even if they were, would you fish in a place where *that* was?"

"But . . . here it is," Malak protested. "You cannot deny your eyes."

"I can deny any of my senses," Akiro replied mildly, "except those of the mind. As for the boat, perhaps someone knew we were coming."

With a gasp the small thief dropped the boat and fishing lines as if they were serpents. He stepped back from them quickly, wiping his palms on his leather jerkin. "The Stygian knows we are coming? Banba's Buttocks!"

"We make a cold camp just the same," Conan said, stepping down from his saddle. "If he does *not* know we are here, there is no point to telling him with a fire."

"We must cross now," Jehnna said. "Now. The key is there, I tell you."

"It will still be there in the morning," the Cimmerian replied. With clear reluctance she took her eyes from the palace for the first time since reaching the beach, her jaw firming determinedly, but he went on before she could speak. "I have as much reason not to delay as have you, Jehnna. We will cross with the dawn."

"The thief is right, child," Bombatta said. He gestured to the lake, its waters blackening as sunlight failed. "Did the boat tip over in that, you could drown before I found you. I cannot risk that."

Jehnna lapsed into sulky silence, and Conan turned his attentions to Malak. "You can go, if you wish. Neither of us reckoned with this Amon-Rama knowing about us. Consider the jewels yours."

"Jewels?" Bombatta echoed, but the two friends ignored him.

Malak took a step toward his horse, then stopped. "Conan, I. . . . If we had a chance, Cimmerian, but he knows we're coming. Balor's Glaring Eye! You heard Akiro."

"I heard," Conan said.

"You are staying?" Malak asked, and Conan nodded. The wiry man sighed. "I cannot travel in these mountains in the night," he muttered. "I will leave in the morning."

"Now that that is settled," Akiro said, climbing from his horse with a groan, "I am hungry." He dug his fists into the small of his back and stretched. "There is dried lamb in the packs. And figs."

A heavy, solemn air hung over everyone as they

set about making camp. The crater had the effect of making each of them grow silent and introspective, all save Jehnna, and she was rapt with the approach to a part of her destiny.

Soon the horses were hobbled, the dried meat and fruit had been consumed, and full night was on them. Jehnna wrapped herself in her blankets, and Zula, to everyone's surprise, sat crosslegged beside the slender girl, crooning soothingly while she fell asleep. Bombatta glowered jealously, but the black woman's fierce glare whenever one of the men came close to Jehnna was enough to make even him keep his distance.

As the full moon rose higher the darkness lessened, for it seemed as if the crater in some fashion trapped and held that canescent glow. The air took on a thick pearlescence of unearthly paleness, where faces could be dimly yet distinctly seen. Conan and Akiro sat alone amid the blanket-swathed mounds that marked where the others slept. They sat, and stared across the dark waters at the palace, shining yet illumining nothing, as a diamond on black velvet shone by holding every glimmer of light.

"This place presses in on me," the Cimmerian said finally. "I cannot like it."

"It is not a place to be liked, except by sorcerers," Akiro replied. He moved his hands before him as if caressing the pale light. "I can sense the flow of power from the very rocks. This is a place where bonds are loosed, and the ties that hold the ordinary whole are undone. Here barriers are weak, and names may summon the dead."

Conan shivered, and told himself there was a chill in the air. "I will be glad to be gone from it, back to Shadizar with the things Taramis seeks."

Suddenly a shriek tore the night, and Jehnna twisted in her blankets, staring with unseeing eyes as she screamed. "No! No! Stop!"

Bombatta leaped from his sleep with tulwar in hand, while Malak cursed and struggled with his blankets, a dagger in each fist. Zula hugged the slender girl to her breast and murmured softly.

Suddenly Jehnna threw her arms about the black woman. Sobs convulsed her. "It was horrible," she wept hoarsely. "Horrible!"

"A dream," Bombatta said, sheathing his blade hastily. He knelt beside the girl and tried to take her from Zula, but she clung even more tightly. "Only a dream, child," he said softly. "Nothing more. Go back to sleep."

Zula glared at him over the girl she held. "Dreams are important. Dreams can tell the future. She must speak of it."

"I agree," Akiro said. "There are often portents in dreams. Speak, Jehnna."

"It was only a dream," Bombatta growled. "Who can say what she might dream in this evil place."

"Speak," Akiro said again to the girl.

Saying the words softly within Zula's comforting arms, Jehnna began. Her dark eyes were still wide with terror. "I was an infant, barely able to walk by myself. I woke and saw my nurse asleep, and I slipped from the nursery. I wanted my mother. Down many corridors I ran, until I came to the room where I knew my mother slept, and my father. Their bed lay in the middle of the floor, and sheer hangings from the ceiling surrounded it. I could see them there, sleeping. And another figure, as well, like a boy. It crouched at the head of the bed, looking down at my mother and my father. The dim light of the lamps gleamed strangely on the figure's hands. One hand raised, and I saw . . . I saw it held a dagger. The dagger fell, and my father made a strange sound, groaning as if he were hurt. My mother woke, then. She screamed a name, and another dagger slashed. There was blood everywhere. I ran. I wanted to scream, but it was as if I had no tongue. All I could do was run and run and run and—"

Zula gave her a fierce shake, then hugged her even closer. "It is all right, Jehnna. You are safe, now. Safe."

"The name," Akiro prompted. "What was the name?"

Jehnna peeked hesitantly out of the circle of Zula's arms. "Taramis," she whispered. "It was Taramis. Oh, why would I dream this? Why?"

No one made a sound until Bombatta said, "A dream of madness. A foul dream brought on by this foul place. Even my sleep is troubled by things that never were."

"So it seems," Akiro said at last. "You will see to her?" he asked Zula.

The ebon woman nodded, and stroked Jehnna's hair as she began again the soft crooning that had brought sleep before. Bombatta sat on the other side of the girl, as if he, too, would guard her sleep this time. The two warriors, man and woman, stared at each other unblinkingly.

In company with Akiro Conan walked slowly to the water's edge, its black sheen undisturbed by the smallest ripple. "When Jehnna was barely old enough to walk," the Cimmerian said slowly, "Taramis was perhaps sixteen. Just barely the age to be invested with her brother's titles and estates."

"Perhaps it was just a dream."

"Perhaps," Conan said. "Perhaps."

Amon-Rama peered into the crimson depths of the Heart of Ahriman, frowning at the sleeping figures. None remained awake on the far side of the night-shrouded lake. Last to slumber had been the yellow-skinned wizard, peering into the sky and attempting—this brought a momentary sneer to the Stygian's hawk nosed face—attempting to touch the powers cupped in the crater. The wizard had retired long after the others breathed deep and slow beneath their blankets. But now even he slept. On the morn they would come, and. . . .

His frown deepened to a scowl. On the morn. Long had he waited, and now there were but hours more to wait, yet he itched with impatience. Naught could go wrong at so late a moment. So why did he feel as if ants crawled on his skin?

He released his concentration from the Heart, and the glow faded, leaving only a gem more scarlet than rubies. He would not spend a night so. There would be an end to it.

Swiftly he strode from the mirrored chamber, through crystal halls whose smallest golden ornament would have been a delight to kings, up to the top of the tallest glittering spire of the palace. From that towering height he looked once toward the far shore, as if his unaided eyes could pierce the unnaturally pale night, then produced from beneath his hooded vermilion robes a black chalk compounded from the burned bones of murdered men and the life's breath of virgins.

In quick strokes he scribed a pentagram, leaving one break so it would be safe for him to enter. In each point of the star he drew two symbols, one the same and one different in each of the five. The like symbols would add their warding to the protective power of the pentagram. The other five would summon. Holding his robes carefully so as to smudge no part of the pattern—there could be disaster in that!—he stepped within, and completed the last segment of the unholy diagram.

Slowly at first, then with greater force, he began to chant, until he howled the words at the night. Yet he heard no word he spoke. Such words were not meant for men. His ear could not hear them. Only with long years of painful practice could he speak them. In that place where bonds were broken, Amon-Rama invoked spirits of change and dissolution.

Bit by bit the paleness of the night seem to gather around him, thickening, swirling, enfolding, hiding him as in a pillar of smoke. And that smoke grew and shaped, changed. Wings stretched forth in a span four times the height of a man. Massive talons scraped at the adamantine crystal of the towertop. Within the scribed lines of power stood a gigantic bird, a fierce-beaked eagle, but all of smoke that swirled and roiled within.

The great wings beat—there was no sound, as if they did not beat at the air of this world—and the monstrous form rose into the night. Swiftly the vaporous creature flew, until it circled far above the black sand beach. Ethereal pinions folded, and the bird-shape swooped.

Unerring it struck, straight at the slender form of the girl. Huge wings smote doward to brake; no flutter of air disturbed the blankets of the black woman or the scar-faced man sleeping on either side. Talons closed firmly about her slender body, but she did not wake, nor give any sign that she felt any other than deep, normal sleep.

Upward the smoky creature flew, then, wings seeming to sweep the breadth of the sky as they hurtled it back across the raven lake to the coruscant spire. As it lowered toward that vitric tower, the bird-form dissolved once more to a pillar of smoke, a pillar that touched down within the pentagram, swirled, and dissipated to reveal Amon-Rama bearing Jehnna in his red-robed arms.

Carefully he scrubbed out a section of the diagram with his foot, then stepped out. The rest he could dispose of later. Now there was a matter more important. The lifeless-eyed necromancer smiled thinly—it touched no more than his lips—down at the lovely face she turned up to him in her unbroken sleep. A matter infinitely more important.

Crystalline stairs that chimed beneath his hurried tread carried him down into the palace. To the chamber of mirrors, he hastened, and beyond, to a room like no other in that sparkling faceted structure, nor like any other to be found on the face of the earth.

Elsewhere in that crystal palace was there always light and brightness, without need of lamp or sun. Here was darkness. The walls seemed tapestried with blackest shadow, if walls there were, or ceiling or floor, for the chamber appeared to extend in all directions infinitely, and no spark of light in it save two. Brightness framed the doorway that gave entrance from the chamber of mirrors, but that brightness failed abruptly at the very door. No pool of light stretched from it. The second light was indeed a pool, a soft glow without apparent source that surrounded a huge bed piled high with silken cushions. On that bed Amon-Rama laid his slight burden.

He looked down at her, no expression in his flat black eyes, then slowly traced one hand along the line from slim ankle to rounded thigh to tiny waist to swelling breast. Normal vices had been burned out of him by his thaumaturgies long years ago, but others remained, others that gave him dark pleasures. And, he thought, as he had not the same use for the girl as that foolish woman, Taramis, there was no reason for him not to indulge himself in them. But when his sport with the others was done. Now that the girl, the One, was finally in his grasp, his impatience was gone. Now was a time for preparations.

"Hear me now!" he called, his voice rolling into vast distances. "No door, no window, no crack nor opening to air. So do I say it, so must it be!"

The crystal palace tolled brazenly like a great bell, and it was so. The palace was sealed.

"Let us see first how they deal with that," he murmured.

With a final glance at Jehnna's unmoving form, he made his way from the place. When he had shut the door behind him, only the one pool of light remained, and Jehnna floated in the midst of infinite dark.

xii

Eerily pearlescent darkness still filled the crater when Conan woke, but he did not need a paling of the sky to the east to tell him that dawn approached. To cross the lake at dawn they must be awake before dawn, therefore he had awakened in good time. It was a useful trick he had, though he would admit that too much wine could befuddle it.

Tossing aside his blankets, he sheathed the bared broadsword that had lain by him through the night and rose, stretching. He frowned as his eye fell on Jehnna's empty blankets. Swiftly he scanned the slope of the crater above their camp. The horses stood with heads down, sleeping. Nothing moved.

He bent to prod Akiro and Malak. "Wake," he said quietly. "Jehnna is gone. Up with you."

Leaving then—Malak spluttering and cursing,

Akiro muttering direly about his age and need for
sleep—Conan strode to where Bombatta and Zula
slept, one to either side of the empty blankets
where Jehnna had been. He glared at the scar-
faced warrior, snoring in a low buzz, and planted
his booted foot in the man's ribs.

With a startled yelp Bombatta came awake. A
heartbeat later he was snarling to his feet, hand
darting to his tulwar. "I will kill you, thief! I—"

"Jehnna is gone," Conan said with grim cold-
ness. "You all but tie her to you, then let her
disappear. She could be dead!"

Bombatta's fury vanished with the first words.
He stared at her blankets as if struck in the head.

"The horses are all here," Malak called.

The ebon-armored man shook himself. "Of
course they are!" he roared. "Jehnna would not
ride away from her destiny."

"Destiny!" Zula sneered. "You call it her
destiny. Why can she not choose her own destiny?"

"If you have done something with her," Bombatta grated, and the black woman bristled back.

"I? I would never harm her! It is you who
think she is a plaything, to be used as you see
fit!"

The scars stood out as white lines across the big
warrior's face. "You diseased she-jackal! I will
carve you—"

"Fight later!" Conan snapped. "Now we must
find Jehnna!"

Tension between the two lessened, but did not

disappear. Bombatta sheathed his half-bared tulwar with a growl deep in his throat, and Zula's lip
curled angrily as she lowered the staff she held in
both hands.

Akiro had knelt by Jehnna's blankets and begun
running his hands over them. Now his lips moved
silently, and his eyes closed. When he opened them
again only dead-white spheres showed. Malak
gagged loudly and turned away.

"The girl was taken by a bird," the old man
announced.

"Old fool," Bombatta muttered, but Akiro continued as if he had not spoken.

"A great bird, a bird of smoke that moved
without sound. It carried her in its talons." His
eyelids dropped, and opened on normal black eyes.

"A fool?" Conan said to Bombatta. "You are
the fool. And me. We should have expected the
Stygian to do something."

"Where did this bird take her?" Zula asked.

Akiro pointed across the lake to the crystal palace.
"There, of course."

"Then we must follow," she said.

Conan nodded wordless agreement. As one he
and Bombatta ran to the hide boat, wrestled it to
the water.

"But it may be ensorceled," Malak protested.
"Akiro said so."

"We must take the chance," Conan replied. He
stood knee deep in the water beside the narrow
vessel. "In! Quickly!"

In a quick scramble they filled the boat, Zula in the middle between Akiro and Malak, Conan and Bombatta on the ends. Paddles in the big men's hands dug furiously at the water, and the slim boat knifed away from the shore.

"Sigyn's Bowl!!" Malak howled abruptly. "I forgot! I am leaving this morning! Turn back!"

Conan did not slow the steady work of his powerful arms and shoulders. "Swim," he said curtly.

The small thief looked at the liquid beneath them and shuddered. "Water is for drinking," he muttered, "when there is no wine."

With neither wind nor wave to hinder and two strong men working the paddles, the hide boat all but flew over the lake. Ripples from its passage spread incredibly far, for no other thing disturbed that glassy surface. The crystal palace loomed before them. Along its border with the water there was a landing, perfectly ordinary except that it, too, seemed carved from a single huge gem. The sun topped the crater's rim as they reached the palace, and the vast structure became a riot of scintillation.

Conan held the boat close to the strange landing while the others clambered out. When he was on the glittering stone as well, he lifted the hide boat from the water. A thief did not last long in Shadizar who failed to plan for his exits and escapes. For now the lake was still, but he would not risk something sweeping the craft away, not until he knew of some other means of leaving that unnatural palace.

The boat secured, he turned his attention to the palace. Smooth, sparkling walls met his eyes. Far to the right and left were the ends of crystal colonnades with tall, fluted columns of pellucid stone. Above rose featureless, vitreous expanses of sheer wall topped by faceted domes and glittering spires stretching toward the sky.

"Fascinating," Akiro murmured, stroking his fingertips over the crystal wall. "There are no joins. It is truly one single gem. All of it. Fascinating."

"Better it were ordinary marble," Conan said roughly. "I could contrive a means to scale that. Come. We must find a doorway of some sort."

"There is none," Akiro said without breaking his abstract reverie.

"How," Conan began, then thought better of asking how the wizard knew there were no doors. "Then how in Zandru's Nine Hells do we get in?" he asked instead.

Akiro blinked in surprise. "Oh, that part is easy." He walked to the edge of the landing and pointed to the water. "Down there is an opening. I could sense it the very first time I tried, perhaps because it is the *only* opening I found. It is big enough for our uses."

"A means of getting water from the lake?" Zula said doubtfully.

"I do not like water," Malak grumbled, but it was the palace he eyed nervously.

Conan knelt beside the round-bellied mage and peered at the water's surface. It was unruffled once more, and he could see nothing but his own image. It could not be possible, he told himself, that this Amon-Rama would build a palace with no way in, then leave such a simple entrance as this. A trap, he thought, with Jehnna for bait. Then let the trapper discover what manner of creature it was he meant to snare. He breathed deeply to flush his lungs with air, and dove into the lake. Only a small splashed marked his entrance

There was a grayish clarity to the water below the surface. The Cimmerian took himself deeper with powerful strokes, searching along the face of the landing. The crystal surface was unmarked by the slimes and green things that grew on normal stonework immersed so.

Quickly he found the opening, a great pipe nearly as wide as his out-stretched arms, with a cross-hatch of thick iron bars across it. Seizing the bars, he braced his feet against the wall beside the pipe and heaved. Nothing gave, not even the slightest. Harder he pulled, till his sinews creaked, and still to no avail. Abruptly he was startled to see other hands beside his own. He looked up and stared into the straining face of Bombatta, stripped of his black armor. Conan threw himself into redoubled effort. Bone and thew quivered, and lungs burned.

Suddenly, with a sharp crack, one bar tore loose

in a shower of jewel-like shards. The grating shifted in Conan's hands, and he found he had more leverage. Crystal splintered and broke, and one by one the other bars came free.

Letting the grate fall, the Cimmerian sped back to the surface. As his head broke water he gulped air. He did not look around when Bombatta surfaced beside him. From the landing's edge three anxious faces peered down.

"The way is open," Conan said between pants. "Come."

"Wait but a moment," Akiro said. "Regain your breath. We must make a plan."

"No time," Conan replied. One last breath he drew, then rolled over and swam downward again.

With a quick twist he turned into the pipe, powerful strokes carrying him deeper. The light faded behind him, and he swam in darkness. Thirty paces, now. Forty, and his lungs demanded air. Fifty. And suddenly there was a glow ahead. Swiftly he swam toward it, then turned upward toward the light's source, moving arms and legs to slow his ascent. He broke the surface with only the sound of a droplet falling.

He was in a well, he saw, walled with the same smooth crystal as made up the palace. A wooden bucket was sunk in the water next to him, its rope pulled taut. Carefully he tugged the rope. It did not give.

A deadly smile came onto his face. Amon-Rama no doubt thought himself secure, and his trap subtle.

In the northlands, though, there was an ancient saying. To trap a Cimmerian is to trap your own death.

Someone surfaced beside him with a splash that echoed from the well's walls, but he did not look to see who it was. He would allow only one thought, now. Grasping the rope, he climbed hand over hand with a grim face. The Cimmerian had entered the trap, and he hunted.

In the chamber of mirrors Amon-Rama thoughtfully tapped his pointed chin with a long, thin finger. They were inside the palace. He had forgotten the pipe that brought water to his well, and they had found his oversight quickly. Good sport was indicated.

With a malevolent smile he lightly touched a mirrored wall. It was not, of course, as if these interlopers had some chance of escape or—all the powers of darkness forfend!—victory. This palace was his in ways no king could dream of. The shriek of the crystal as the bars were torn free. That had come to him. The tread of their feet in the corridors, the disturbing of the air by their breath, all came to him. But then, he found sport in other ways than offering true hope to his prey. Their false belief in false hope sufficed, and even greater sport came when all hope was stripped away.

Now was time for preparations. He spoke a word, raised his hands, and the golden draperies shrouding the walls rolled neatly upwards revealing the five score great mirrors that surrounded the chamber. Each mirror reflected the clear plinth that held the glowing Heart of Ahriman, but none showed Amon-Rama. A lifetime drenched in darkest thaumaturgies had many peculiar effects on the earthly body of the practitioner. He *had* no reflection to be shown in any surface.

Only two breaks were there in the phalanx of mirrors. One was the door to the corridor. Through the other he could see endless dark and the bed on which Jehnna's still sleeping form lay. It was through this last that Amon-Rama moved. A sound rolled round the chamber, like the splash of a rock in a pool of water, and there was but a single gap unmirrored in the wall. Five score and one reflections of the Heart of Ahriman waited with the original.

Akiro pulled himself from the well with a grunt and, ignoring the water that dripped from him, stood staring at gem-like walls and ornaments of gold and silver so finely wrought that it seemed the mind of man could not have conceived them. Everywhere were tapestries of other-worldly scenes and carpets that changed in infinite variety of color and pattern as he watched.

"Akiro?" Malak said.

The rotund wizard shook his head admiringly. All done with sorcery; no one of these things had ever been crafted by a human hand. It was magnificent.

"Akiro?"

Irritably the mage turned to regard the small thief. Malak's hair hung in his face, and a pool of water about his feet splashed with a rain of drops from his garments. He looked like a drowned rat, Akiro thought, then quickly scrubbed his own dripping hair from his face. "Yes?" he snapped.

"They are going," Malak said.

Akiro looked in the direction the other pointed, and bit back an oath that would have curdled the air. Bombata and Zula were disappearing around a bend in the corridor, and Conan was no longer to be seen. "Fools," he muttered. "Wait!" As swiftly as he could make his old bones move, he ran after them, with Malak dogging his heels. "Half-wits!" the old mage growled. "You do not wander about a wizard's lair as if it were a merchant's garden! Here, anything can happen!"

As he rounded the corner, Akiro saw the others ahead, with Conan far in the lead. Sword in hand, the Cimmerian darted through a doorway at the end of the corridor, and in the same instant a door slid down with a clang, sealing the passage behind him. Bombatta and Zula rushed forward to pound on the door, he with his sword hilt, she with her staff.

Cursing under his breath Akiro ran to help, but for moments after reaching them he could only stare. The door was as transparent as glass—clearly they could see Conan, looking warily about a mirrored chamber, his broadsword at the ready—yet the blows of Bombatta and Zula rebounded as if from an iron-bound castle gate. As if to add to the hollow booming, all began to shout at once.

"Can he not hear us?" Malak cried. "Conan! Ogun's Toenails! Conan!"

Zula dropped to her knees, feeling along the bottom of the door. "If we can lift . . . there is no crack! None!"

"Stand back," Bombatta roared, taking a two-handed grip on his sword. "I'll break it if it can be broken."

"*All* of you stand back," Akiro shouted over them. "And be quiet," he added. He rummaged in his pouch, sighing as he tossed aside powders ruined by the wet, yet continued to speak hastily the while. "This is no tavern brawl, to be settled with brute might. This Stygian is a sorcerer of puissance. Treat him as such, or we will all . . . ah, here it is." Smiling in satisfaction, he brought out a small vial covered entirely with purest beeswax and marked with a seal of power.

"I do not see Jehnna," Bombatta said suddenly. "The thief must be left to his fate. Jehnna must be found."

"She is here," Akiro said, not looking up from the task of peeling away the wax. The peeling must be done properly, or the contents would be useless. "Can you not sense . . . of course you cannot. The nexus is here, the center of all the powers of this palace.''

The last of the wax fell away, revealing a darkly shimmering compound that seemed at once grease and smoke. To this he touched the tip of the smallest finger of his left hand, and scribed a rune on the right-hand side of the transparent door. With the smallest finger of his right hand he drew the same symbol on the left-hand side of the door.

Akiro frowned as the runes began to hiss, as if boiling, but there was nothing to be done for it. Quickly he began to chant in silence. There were powers invoked with words spoken aloud, but he had found those dangerous, unreliable or foul, and often all three. Pressure built; he could feel it inside his head. They were spirits he summoned, spirits concerned with opening things that could not be opened, spirits concerned with lifting what could not be lifted. The pressure grew, and he knew they obeyed the calling. The pressure grew, and sweat beaded on his forehead. The pressure grew, and grew, and. . . .

With a gasp, he slumped and would have fallen had he not caught himself against the door.

''Well?'' Bombatta demanded.

Shaking, Akiro stared at the door in wonder. The pressure was still there, enough to burst the gate of a castle, and to no effect. ''A wizard most puissant,'' he whispered, then added as he peered into the mirrored chamber, ''If you believe in gods, then pray.''

xiii

Slowly Conan moved around the mirrored chamber, broadsword held ready for any attack. The huge mirrors cast back his stalking form, multiplied ten thousand times as reflections of reflections were in turn reflected, and that of the glowing crimson gem that stood on a slim crystalline spire in the center of the room. Without break was the wall of grim images, and he realized that he was no longer certain which had fallen to hide the door through which he had entered.

He had avoided the gem before. The glow and its color told him all he needed of its nature. Never had he seen anything so scarlet; the hue alone made him want to squint. Such items of sorcerous power were dangerous when not understood—as he had learned in hard lessons—and scarcely less so when comprehension was complete. Still, it was the only thing in the chamber other than himself. Slowly he approached the narrow plinth, and stretched forth a hand.

"You provide little sport, barbarian."

Spinning, the big Cimmerian searched for the source of the words, and when he found it he was hardly less surprised than at hearing them in the first place.

One tall mirror no longer depicted him, but rather a man in hooded, blood-red robes. At least, he assumed it was a man from the voice and the size. The deep hood hid the face in shadow, while the robe hung in vermilion folds to the floor and even the hands were covered by long sleeves that depended to points.

"I will provide no sport at all for you, Stygian," Conan said. "Release the girl, or—"

"You become tiresome." A score of voices behind him spoke the words, and all were the Stygian's voice. Suspecting some form of trick to divert him, Conan risked a glance back. And stared. Twenty mirrors now held the hooded form.

"I will keep the girl, and you can do nothing."

"She is the One, and the One is mine."

"Muscles and steel avail you naught against *my* power."

Conan felt as if his head were whirling. Each time there were more scarlet-robed images in the mirrors, chorusing the words, until he was surrounded by the mage, multiplied more than a hundred times. Hairs on his arms and the back of his neck stirred, and his teeth bared in a snarl. Yet many times had he met fear, and that stealer of will and strength was as familiar to him as the dark form of death. If the latter would one day surely conquer him, the former had no power he had not defeated a thousand times before.

"You think to frighten me, sorcerer? I spit on your power, for you hide behind it like a cowering dog. You have not the courage to face me like a man."

"Brave words," the multitudinous reflections murmured in oily tones. "Perhaps I shall face you." Abruptly two of the images split in twain. From each of those mirrors one shape streaked in a blur of scarlet; the two blurs struck, merged, and the shape of the mage stood at one end of the chamber as well as in the mirrors. "Perhaps you will give some small sport, after all. You will not like it, barbar. I will kill you slowly, and you will scream for death long before it comes. Your strength will be as that of a child against me."

With every word more of the mirrored forms divided, more flashes of crimson blazed across the chamber to sink into the hooded figure, and with each the figure grew slightly larger.

Twice, as blood-red streaks passed close to him, Conan struck at them with his sword. The steel whistled through them as through the air, with only a tingling along his arms to tell him the blade had met anything. The Cimmerian stood then, waiting rather than waste his effort in futility, until at last each mirror had given up its portion of the red-robed form that faced him. Taller than he by a head, it was, and twice as broad.

"This you call facing me?" Conan sneered. "Well, come then."

The huge shape stripped back its hood, and as Conan started in spite of himself, hundred-fold laughter rolled from the mirrors. An ape's head glared at him from atop the scarlet robes, as black as pitch and with gleaming white fangs made for the ripping of flesh. Its eyes held malevolent ebon fire. A tiger's claws tipped its thick, hairy fingers. Slowly it shredded the robes, revealing a massive, ebon-haired body and heavy, bowed legs. No sound came from it, not even that of breathing.

A creation of sorcery it most certainly was, Conan thought, but perhaps it still could bleed. With a roar he bounded the length of the chamber, his broadsword a razor-edged windmill. Like a leopard the creature danced away from him, moving faster than he would have believed anything of that bulk could possibly move. And even in its dodging it struck—almost casually, it seemed—opening four crimson-welling slashes across his chest.

Grimly Conan followed. Three more times he struck at the great beast. Three more times, with silent snarls, it avoided his steel like quicksilver, and blood now dripped from his thigh, his shoulder, and his forehead. Full-throated laughter flowed from the mirrors in counterpoint to the frustrated curses the Cimmerian muttered under his breath. The creature's every move was lightning, exhibiting none of the clumsiness of its shape. He had not so much as touched it yet.

Abruptly the monstrous sable ape charged, seized him in an instant, lifted him toward that slathering fanged mouth. He was too close to hack or stab with his sword, yet he slashed his blade sideways across the snarling face, slicing a gash through eye and nose and mouth. Claws dug into his ribs as green ichor rose in the wound, and the one remaining bulged in agony. With a heave of its massive arms Conan was sent hurtling across the chamber.

It could be hurt, flashed through the Cimmerian's mind, and then he slammed into the wall, all the air leaving his lungs, and slid to the floor. Desperately he struggled to breathe, fought to regain his feet before the beast could reach him. He staggered to his feet . . . and stared in amazement.

The huge ape had sunk to all fours, and its mouth hung open as if it would moan if it were not mute. Yet that agonized sound was supplied a hundred times over by the images of the mage. In every mirror the form of the necromancer sagged and groaned in pain.

Not in every mirror, Conan realized suddenly. The mirror he had struck in his flight was crossed by a web of cracks and showed only shattered reflections, including, now, his own once more. He swung his blade against the next mirror. As the silvery surface fragmented beneath the blow, the figure of Amon-Rama within vanished, and the groans of the others became cries.

"I have you, sorcerer!" Conan shouted above the shrill ululations.

Along the wall he ran as fast as he could, pausing only to smash at each mirror as he passed. Image after image of the thaumaturge disappeared to the splintering of glass, to cries becoming howls, then shrieks.

The skittering of claws on the crystal floor warned the Cimmerian, and he threw himself into a roll just as the ape-creature lunged at him. His broadsword flashed as he came to his feet. A gash ran down the beast's ribs, while he had gained another along his own ribs. It was slower, he thought; no faster, now, than a fast man. Still, he ran across the chamber, ignoring the monstrous form. Defeating the creature was no part of defeating Amon-Rama.

At the far wall Conan stabbed his sword viciously at the image of the necromancer in mirror after mirror. The screams now spoke of pain beyond knowing, and of desperation, as well. From the corner of his eye, Conan saw the huge ape scrambling toward him again, its lone black eye burning with a frantic light. Yet even in its haste, he noted, it circled wide around the glowing red gem.

Abruptly, with a splashing sound as if he had stabbed into water, Conan's sword pierced the surface of a mirror. He could only stare. His blade went *into* the mirror, and into, as well, the image of Amon-Rama within. Silence was thick in the chamber, broken only by an occasional tinkling as a bit of broken mirror fell to the crystal floor. All of the unbroken mirrors save the one his sword transfixed now showed only normal reflections. The ape-beast was gone as if it had never been, though the burning of his gashes told him it most assuredly had been real.

Beneath the scarlet hood in the mirror a hawk-nosed face was painted with disbelief, and raven eyes shone hatred at the big youth. A ball of light suddenly oozed from the place where the blade entered the mage's robes, flowed down the sword and exploded, hurling Conan away like a flung stone. Shaking his head, the Cimmerian got dazedly to his feet just as Amon-Rama stepped out of the mirror, its surface first bulging around him, then suddenly vanishing into vapor.

The necromancer did not look at Conan. Once he touched the sword that thrust from his chest as if to convince himself of its actuality. With staggering steps he moved toward the crimson gem atop its slim pelucid column.

"Cannot be," the Stygian muttered. "All power would have been mine. All power. . . ."

His hand closed about the glowing stone, and the wail that ripped from him then, going on as if it would never end, made all the other sounds he had uttered pale to whispers. Scarlet light glared from between his fingers, brighter and brighter, until it seemed that his hand itself had taken on the color.

"Crom!" Conan whispered as he realized the hand *had* become crimson.

And the redness spread, up the sorcerer's arm and through him, till he was as a statue of congealed blood, yet keening still. Abruptly the form collapsed into a sanguinary pool that boiled and bubbled, vermilion steam rising till naught was left save his broadsword lying on the crystal floor. And the gem, hanging unsupported in the air.

Carefully, with more than one hesitant glance at the crimson stone floating above his blade, Conan retrieved his weapon. The leather-wrapped hilt was hot in his hand, but the sword seemed unharmed. Swiftly he backed away from the sorcerous stone, and his skin crawled. Almost had he touched the accursed thing, before Amon-Rama began his fatal game.

With a deafening crash another of the mirrors burst, and Conan's companions poured into the chamber.

". . . and I told you it would work," Akiro was saying. "It took only the death of the sorcerer, releasing his hold on his majicks."

"Ravana's Weeping Eyes," Malak said scornfully. "You said he was lucky. There was no luck. This Stygian should have known better than to oppose Malak and Conan."

Akiro turned his attention to the Cimmerian. "You *were* lucky. One day your luck will run out like the sands from a glass, and what then?"

"You saw?" Conan asked, now that he could get a word in edgewise.

Akiro nodded, and Zula shivered. "That ape," she murmured, looking about as if she suspected it might only be hiding.

"It is gone," Conan said. "Let us find Jehnna and this Mitra-accursed key, and be gone as well."

As though her name had summoned her Jehnna appeared, stepping through the gap left by the mirror from which Amon-Rama had come. Behind her was blackness made darker by the glittering crystal and mirrors in the chamber. She did not look at any of them, but walked slowly, surely, to the radiant red gem, hanging still where the Stygian sorcerer had left it.

"No!" Conan and Bombatta shouted together, but before either man could move she plucked the stone from the air.

"The Heart of Ahriman," she said softly, smiling at the blood-red jewel in her hand. "This is the key, Conan."

"That?" Conan began, then cut off as a tremor shook the floor. The walls shivered, and ominous crackings sounded.

"I should have known," Akiro mused. "It was Amon-Rama's will that held it, and with him dead—" Abruptly he stopped to glare at the others. "Well? Did you not hear me? Run, or we are all as dead as the Stygian!" As if for punctuation another quaver ran through the palace.

"The well!" Conan commanded, though the

thought of that swim with the possibility that the palace might collapse atop them all was not one he enjoyed.

Akiro shook his head. "Allow me to show what I can do without the interference of Amon-Rama." He gave Malak a significant look. "Watch." Chanting silently, he moved his arms in strange patterns—it looked to Conan much like what he had seen at the wizard's camp, yet in some fashion different—clapped his hands, and a fiery sphere shot from between his palms to strike a mirrored wall. There was no eruption, this time. Rather the ball of the fire spread and hollowed, like the flames of a hot coal touched to parchment. In only a moment it extinguished, leaving behind a roughly circular doorway melted in the crystal wall. "There," Akiro said. "Now, Malak, have you seen anything to surpass—"

This time the palace danced and swayed, and a portion of another crystalline wall fell with a shattering crash.

"We'll talk of our triumphs later," Conan said, grabbing Jehnna's arm. The others hesitated not a moment in following him through the way Akiro had provided.

Down glittering corridors of ethereal beauty they ran, and when the corridor bent away from the direction they wished to go Akiro melted yet another hole in the sparkling crystal walls. Faster and faster the shocks came, until they blended into one continuous gyration of the entire palace. Ornaments of unearthly exquisiteness burst apart, walls toppled in bounding chunks of pellucid stone, and twice entire stretches of the ceiling fell in solid blocks behind them.

Then Akiro's magic burned its way through yet again, and they rushed out onto the landing. The lake was in turmoil, choppy waves radiating out from the palace. Conan heaved the hide boat, heavier for Bombatta's armor already lashed in its bottom, to the water, handed Jehnna into it, then had to hold the craft against the scar-faced warrior's attempt to push off before the others could scramble aboard.

When all were in, Conan leaped into the boat and snatched up a paddle. "Now," he growled at Bombatta. The other man dug his paddle in without speaking.

Behind them the crystal palace scintillated with all the hues of the rainbow gone mad. Lightnings leaped from tall spires, *up* into cloudless skies.

"Faster," Akiro urged, staring anxiously over his shoulder. "Faster!" He glared at Conan and Bombatta, wielding their paddles with all their might, and grunted. Trailing his hands in the water, the wizard began to chant, and slowly the water mounded beneath the boat. Swelling, the wave rushed forward, carrying the frail vessel faster than all their stroking could have. Malak loudly tried to pray his way through all known pantheons.

"Too much magic," Conan grumbled.

"Perhaps," Akiro replied, "you would rather wait until that palace—"

With a roar like the rending of the earth the crystal palace burst asunder. A hammering wind smote their backs, and then the wave they rode was caught and overwhelmed by a greater wave. Bow down at a precipitous angle, the hide craft hurtled across the lake. All Conan could do was dig in his paddle and hope to hold them straight. Did they turn sideways to that wall of water, all was lost.

The beach of black sand approached at incredible velocity, then disappeared beneath the wave. Abruptly the bow of the boat struck against the crater's slope, and the vessel cartwheeled, catapulting them all into frothing water.

Conan struggled to his feet, fighting the water's attempt to pull his legs from under him. Jehnna, floundering, swept by him, and he seized a handful of her robes and pulled her to him. She flung one arm around his neck and clung to him, panting, as the water rushed away, leaving them standing a quarter of the way up the slope of the crater.

"Are you all right?" he asked her.

She nodded, then held up the hand not clutching him. "And I did not lose the key." A crimson glow seeped between her fingers.

The Cimmerian shivered, and did not try to stop her when she moved away from him. From beneath her dripping robes she produced a black velvet bag into which she slipped the gem.

Conan shook his head. The longer this journey went on, the less he wanted to do with it. And yet—his hand closed around the golden amulet at his neck, the amulet Valeria had given him—and yet there were reasons.

He was surprised to realize that all of the party were not only alive but on their feet, if soaked and bedraggled, and staring at one another in disbelief that they still lived. Fear had apparently driven the horses despite their hobbles, for they stood, whickering nervously, higher still on the slope. The boat lay below them, and from there to the water were scattered the remains of their camp, such as was left. The cooking pot was gone, and half the waterbags, and a single blanket remained tangled in the rushes.

On the far side of the lake the only sign that the palace had ever been was a vast hole which the waters of the lake were quickly filling. Akiro stared toward it with something approaching sadness on his face. "All a creation of his will," he said quietly. "It was magnificent."

"Magnificent?" Zula's voice squeaked with incredulity. "Magnificent?"

"I would as soon be far away from it," Jehnna said. "And I can sense the treasure, now that I hold the key." At that Bombatta hurried to her, hovering protectively and glaring at Zula and Conan as if the greatest danger came from them.

Malak rubbed his hands together, and lowered his voice for the Cimmerian's ear alone. "Treasure.

I like the sound of that better than wizards. We will help ourselves to whatever the girl does not want, eh? Soon we'll be in Shadizar, living like kings.''

"Soon," Conan agreed. His eyes on Jehnna were troubled, and his hand tightened on the amulet until the golden dragon dug into his palm. "Soon."

XIV

It was possible, Conan reflected as he rode southward, that Akiro's cures were worse than the wounds they were meant to heal. Gray-flanked mountains reared about him, cut with a hundred narrow valleys that could serve as roads for attack and an endless string of pinched passes where ambush could blossom in blood, but he found it hard to keep his mind on anything but the bandages, smeared with foul-smelling ointment, that covered the gashes the ape-creature had opened. Worse than the stench, they itched with a fury. Surreptitiously he scratched at the linen folds wrapped around his chest.

"Do not do that," Jehnna said briskly. "Akiro says they must not be disturbed."

"They are foolishness," Conan grumbled. "I

have had scratches such as these before. Wash the blood off, then let the air to them. That's all I ever needed before.''

"They are *not* scratches," she said firmly.

"And this grease stinks."

" 'Tis a pleasant herbal smell. I begin to wonder if you have sense enough to take care of yourself." She went on, oblivious to his dumbfounded stare. "You will leave your bandages alone. Akiro says that his ointment will heal your wounds completely in only two days. He said I must keep an eye on you, but truly I did not believe it.''

Conan twisted in his high-pommeled saddle to glare back at the wispy-haired wizard. Akiro met his stare calmly, and the others were watching him as well. Malak and Zula wore looks of smug amusement. Bombatta seemed lost in thought, but his eyes rested on Conan in a fashion that made it clear he would not have wept had the ape-inflicted gashes proved fatal.

"I must say you do not seem grateful," Jehnna continued. "Akiro labors to make you well, and you—"

"Mitra's Mercies, girl," Conan said abruptly "do you have to go on so?"

Hurt clouded her face, and the look in her big eyes made him feel it was his fault. "Forgive me," she said shortly, and let her mount fall back. Malak replaced her.

"Sometimes," Conan told the small thief, "I

think I liked that girl more when she was affrighted of her own shadow.''

"I like them with more to fill the arm," Malak said, and flinched at the Cimmerian's cold gaze. "Ah, look you, it's not the girl I want to talk of. Do you know where we are?"

Conan nodded. "I know."

"Then why are you not turning another way? Inti put his hand over us! Another league at most, and we'll be getting close to the village where we found Zula." The wiry man made a sound half sigh and half groan. "They'll not be glad to see us again, Cimmerian. It will be luck if we get no more than a fistful of arrows from ambush."

"I know," Conan said again. He looked back at Jehnna. She rode with her head down and the hood of her pale cloak pulled far forward to hide her face. Every line of her spoke of a deep sulk. "Must we ride all the way back to the village?" he called.

Jehnna jerked erect, blinking. "What? The village?" She looked around, then pointed to the east, to a strait pass rising between two dark, snow-capped peaks. "We must go that way."

"Praise all the gods," Malak breathed, and at that moment two-score mounted Corinthian soldiers burst upon them with longswords gleaming in their fists.

Conan wasted no wind on curses; he had not a moment for it in any case. His broadsword came into his hand barely in time to block an overhand strike that would have split his skull. He kicked a foot free of its stirrup to boot another Corinthian in red-crested helm from his saddle, and as if it were all one motion slashed open his first attacker's throat. He saw Malak bend beneath a flashing blade to sink his dagger under the bottom of a polished breastplate, then another cavalryman was upon him.

"Conan!" The shrill scream reached him even as he engaged. "Conan!"

The one glance the Cimmerian could spare was enough to freeze the breath in his throat. A laughing soldier had his hand tangled in Jehnna's dark hair, and their two horses danced in a circle, only her frantic grip on the tall pommel of her saddle keeping her from being unseated.

One glance Conan could spare, and when his eyes turned back to his opponent the Corinthian gasped at what he saw in those icy sapphires, for it was his own death. The man was no mean hand with his long cavalry sword, but he had no chance against the grim northland fury he faced now. Thrice their blades met, then Conan was turning away from a bloody corpse that toppled to the rocky ground behind him.

Desperately Conan raced his horse for Jehnna. The slender girl had loosed one hand from her saddle to clutch at the first in her hair; her other hand had only a precarious, clawed hold on the pommel. The horses pranced and circled, and the Corinthian threw back his head in gales of laughter.

"Erlik take you, dog!" Conan snarled, and stood in his stirrups so that his backhand blow had all the strength of his massive body driving the whipping blade.

So great was his rage that he barely felt the shock as his razor steel sheared through the laughing soldier's neck. Mouth frozen forever in mirth the Corinthian's head flew from his shoulders; blood fountained from a torso that remained erect for moments longer, then rolled over the rump of the prancing horse. Fingers twisted in Jehnna's hair almost pulled her from her saddle before they slackened in death. She slumped across the pommel, sobbing wildly and staring with bulging eyes at the headless body beneath her horse's hooves.

It took Conan no more than an instant to take in the situation on the small battlefield. Malak now rode one of the smaller, Corinthian horses, and even as the Cimmerian looked he leaped from that to another, pulling back the rider's head by the red crest on his helmet and slitting his throat. Flashes and roars accompanied Akiro on his mad dashes about the narrow valley. Every time the rotund wizard found time to breathe he began the arm motions that heralded his major displays of power, but each time horsemen in polished breastplates would close about him and, with a shouted curse, Akiro would startle them with a burst of light and a clap of thunder. The deflagrations and deafening bangs hurt no one, though, and the old man was finding less time after each to try his greater wizardries. Zula and Bombatta each attempted to fight to Jehnna's side, but flashing tulwar and whirling staff were hard pressed simply to keep back the soldiers who strove to cut them down.

In the first fury of battle the very numbers of the Corinthians made it inevitable that the balance of dead would favor the Zamorans, but there were simply too many riders in red-crested helms. And dying bravely and stupidly when there were alternatives was one custom of the cities that had never found favor with Conan.

"Scatter!" he roared. Two cavalrymen closed with the big Cimmerian; his blade swept in a circle, severing a swordarm at the elbow, axing deep into the second man's shoulder. He wrenched his steel free without slackening his bellow. "Scatter! They are too many! Scatter!" Seizing Jehnna's reins, Conan booted his horse toward the narrow pass she had indicated as the way they must go.

Three Corinthians spurred to put themselves in the fugitives' way. Surprised grins of anticipation blossomed on their faces when Conan did not wheel in another direction; the grins turned to consternation when the Cimmerian galloped straight into them, his tall Zamoran mount bowling over a smaller animal. The Corinthian screamed as his thrashing horse rolled atop him, grinding him into the stony ground.

Stunned, the pair remaining fell back on defending themselves rather than attacking. Burdened with pulling Jehnna's mount behind him, Conan knew he would have been hardpressed at best to fight a way past. Cold and methodically deadly, he taught them of their fatal mistake. He rode on from two fresh corpses—and one Corinthian screaming and coughing frothy blood—with eyes locked on the narrow pass, eyes as grim as death.

He could not afford to look back, and the knowledge gnawed at him. What if he did look back, and saw one of the others in need? He could not ride back to help. Jehnna must be gotten to the treasure, then to Shadizar with treasure and key, for Valeria. And even without Valeria, he knew he could not abandon the girl. She would get her throat cut, or be dragged behind a boulder by a cavalryman who thought it safe to ignore the unequal fight for a time. Teeth clenching till his jaw ached, he rode, and tried not to hear the sounds of battle fading behind.

XV

The valleys were purple with the shadows of mountains when finally Conan drew rein. He had not galloped all that time—the horses could not have stood such a pace for so long on flat ground, let alone in a maze of twisting valleys—but the animals could not travel forever even at a sensible speed. Besides, he was of a mind to find a place for the night before it was too dark to see.

He glanced back at Jehnna, to see how she was bearing up. The slender girl's cheeks were stained with dust and tear-tracks, and she was sunk in the wide-eyed silence with which she had first greeted him. She held to her saddle with both hands, and showed no more desire to take her own reins now than she had at any time during their flight. She had replied to his few comments only with shakes or nods of her head, though he reluctantly admitted his gruffness of the past few hours might have had something to do with that. All she appeared to want to do was stare at him, and it was beginning to make him nervous. If being in the middle of a battle had driven her mad. . . .

"Are you all right?" he demanded roughly. "Well? Speak to me, girl!"

"You were . . . terrible," she said softly. "They might as well have held switches instead of swords."

"It was not a sport," he muttered, "not the game you still seem to think it." Wondering why he suddenly felt so angry, he resumed looking for a place for camp.

"It is just that I have never seen such a thing before," she continued. "What Zula did, in the village, what happened at Akiro's hut, they were different. I . . . I was apart from them. They were like entertainments, like jugglers or a dancing bear."

He could not help growling his reply. "Men died in those . . . entertainments. Better that they should die than we should, but that does not change the fact of it. No man should die for entertainment." He saw a likely spot, half a score boulders, taller than a man on horseback, set close together and near to a steep slope. Twitching his reins, he turned toward them.

"I did not mean to offend you, Conan."

"I am not offended," he replied sharply.

He led her horse between two of the boulders, just far apart enough to admit him, and found a space between the great stones and the precipitous slope that was more than large enough for them and the animals. The boulders would keep off the worst of the mountain winds and, more importantly, shield them from searchers. Dismounting, he helped Jehnna down and set about unsaddling the horses.

"Build a fire," she said, hugging her cloak about her. "I am cold."

"No fire." Even had there been anything to burn he would not have risked giving away their hiding place. "Here," he said, and tossed the saddle blankets at her.

"They smell," she sniffed, but as he squatted to check their meager supplies he saw that she had draped them about her shoulders over the cloak of white wool, albeit with much wrinkling of her nose.

He had had a waterskin and a pouch of dried meat tied behind his saddle, and there was enough of the meat for several days. Water, however, could be a problem. The skin was only half full.

"Do you think they got away, too?" she asked suddenly. "Bombatta, I mean, and Zula, and the others?"

"Perhaps." Abruptly he tore the bandage from his head, and began unwinding the one about his chest.

"No!" Jehnna cried. "You must leave them. Akiro says—"

"Akiro and the others could be dead because of these," he growled. "Because of me." He used the bandages to wipe off the wizard's greasy ointment. To his surprise the gashes were only slightly swollen pink lines, as if they had had days of healing already. "I was worrying about these, about the itching and the stink. If I had had my mind about me those Corinthians would never have been able to take us by surprise so easily." With an oath he tossed the wadded cloth aside.

"It was not your fault," she protested. "It was me. I was sulking like a child when I should have been telling you the way to go. Had I not been, we would have turned aside before they attacked us."

Conan shook his head. " 'Tis foolishness, Jehnna. In this twisted maze you could have seen the true way but moments sooner, at best, and the Corinthians would have attacked as soon as we turned away from them." He chewed on a strip of dried mutton, as tough as ill-tanned leather and of equal taste, while she frowned pensively.

"Perhaps I could not have done anything more," she said at last, "but I see your point concerning yourself. You, of course, can see around corners and through stone, and so should have warned us. It is quite wonderful to know we had two wizards in our party. But why did you not give us wings, so we could fly away?"

Conan choked on a bit of mutton. Regaining his breath, he glared at her, but she looked back as a wide-eyed vision of innocence. It was possible, he thought, that she was innocent enough to mean exactly what she said, to actually believe that he. . . . No! He was not fool enough to believe that of anyone. He opened his mouth for a retort, and closed it again with the certainty that anything he said would only end in making him feel truly the fool.

"Eat," he said sourly, throwing the pouch of dried meat at her feet.

She chose a piece delicately. He could not be sure, but he thought, as she nibbled at it with small white teeth, that he detected the edges of a smile. It did little for his disposition.

Light faded from the sky, and amethyst twilight descended on the mountains. Finishing the meager meal, Jehnna began to shift about as if seeking for a more comfortable spot on the stony ground. She hitched the blankets this way and that, finally complaining, "I am cold, Conan. Do something."

"No fire," he said curtly. "You have the blankets."

"Well, get beneath them with me, then. If you'll not allow me a fire, at least you can share the warmth of your body."

Conan stared. More innocent than any child, he thought. "I cannot. That is, I will not."

"Why not?" she demanded. "I am freezing. Did not my aunt send you along to protect me?"

Conan laughed and groaned at the same time. Ask the wolf to protect the sheepfold. He shook his head to rid it of unwanted thoughts. "You must have a care of Taramis, Jehnna, when you are back in Shadizar."

"Of my aunt? But why?"

"I have no true reason," he said slowly. "But kings and queens, princes and princesses, do not think as do ordinary folk. They do not see right or wrong the same way."

"Are you troubled by the dream I had? Bombatta was right. It was just a dream, Conan. Anyone could have bad dreams in a place like that crater. Taramis loves me. She has cared for me since I was a child."

"Be that as it may, Jehnna, should you ever have need for help, send word to the tavern of Abuletes, in Shadizar, and I will come. I know many places where you would be safe."

"I will," she said, but he knew she did not believe in even the possibility of it. "I am still cold," she went on, smiling and lifting a corner of one blanket.

A moment longer the big Cimmerian hesitated. Then, telling himself that it was indeed becoming colder, that a sharing of warmth could harm nothing, he removed his sword belt and seated himself next to her. She pulled not only a saddle blanket, smelling strongly of horse, over his shoulders, but part of her cloak as well. The blankets began to slide from them, and as they shifted to secure them he realized that she was leaning against him. Instinctively he put an arm around her. His hand landed on the warm curve of her hip, jumped away as if burned, brushed the soft roundness of a breast, then settled on the indentation of her waist.

" 'Tis warmer than I thought," he muttered. There was sweat on his forehead. "Perhaps I should move." How much forbearance, he wondered, could even the gods ask of a man?

Jehnna snuggled herself more firmly against him, touching the golden dragon at his chest with a single finger. "Tell me of Valeria." He stiffened, and she glanced up at him. "I overheard you and Malak. And Akiro. I am not deaf, Conan. What kind of woman was she?"

"A woman," he replied. But the off-handedness of that would not let him leave it. "She was a woman in thousands upon thousands, perhaps the only one of her kind in the world. She was a warrior, friend, companion. . . ."

". . . And lover?" she supplied when he let his words trail off. He drew breath, but she hurried on before he could speak. "Can there be room in your life for another woman?"

How to explain about Valeria and him, he thought. Valeria, a woman who would neither own nor be owned, a woman who could come to his bed with the passion of a tigress and two hours later nudge him so he did not miss eyeing a particularly toothsome serving wench. "There are things about men and women," he found himself saying, "that you simply would not understand, girl."

"Much you know," she retorted hotly. "Zula

and I had long talks about the proper methods of . . . of handling a man.''

Abruptly she seized his free hand and thrust it beneath her robes. Involuntarily he cupped a warm, hard-tipped mound. The thought returned to him, made to nestle in the palms of a man's hands.

''You know not what you are doing,'' he said hoarsely.

Before the words were out of his mouth she threw herself on him. So great was his surprise that he toppled over backwards, so that she lay atop him.

''Then show me,'' she murmured, and honey lips drove rational thoughts from his head.

The cold night wind swept hard out of the plain across Shadizar, as if seeking to scour the city of its corruption.

It was an omen that the wind blew so, Taramis thought. A symbol of the sweeping away of old ways, and the coming of a new dawn. Her robes of sky blue slashed with gold had been chosen as well to speak of that new sunrise, that inexorable new coming.

Her dark eyes surveyed the courtyard, the largest in her palace. Tiled with huge blocks of pale, polished marble, it was surrounded by an alabaster colonnade. The balconies overlooking the court were empty, and no light showed at any window. Guards within the palace made sure no slave's curious eye fell on what occurred there this night.

Before her rested the great form of Dagoth on its couch of crimson marble. More perfect than any mere mortal male born of woman, she thought. In a circle about her and the massive shape of the Sleeping God stood the priests of the new religion, of the ancient religion reborn. Shimmering golden robes covered the priests to their sandled feet, and on each head was a golden crown with a single point above the brow graven with an open eye, symbol that though the god slept, never did they sleep in his service.

The crown with the tallest point was on the head of he who stood by her right hand, his snowy beard fanning over his chest, his parchment-skinned face the very picture of kindly mildness. His tall staff of gold was topped with a blue diamond carved into an eye of twice human size. He was Xanteres, the high priest. And highest indeed he was, Taramis thought, after herself.

'' 'Tis the third night,'' she said suddenly, and a sigh as of exultation rose from the circle of priests. ''The third night from the Night of Awakening.''

''Blessed be the Night of Awakening,'' intoned the priests.

''The Sleeping God will never die,'' she called, and their reply came back to her.

''Where there is faith, there is no death!''

Taramis held her arms straight out to either side. ''Let us anoint our god with the first of his anointings.''

"All glory to she who anoints the Sleeping God," they chanted.

Flutes began to play, softly and slowly at first, then quickening, rising higher. Two more crowned priests appeared from the collonade. Between them was a girl, her raven hair pinned in tight coils about her small head, her body swathed in robes of pristine white. At the circle the two priests slipped the robes from her, and she entered, unashamed in her slender nakedness. Her eyes, on the form of Dagoth, bore a look of purest rapture as she stopped at the god's head. Taramis and Xanteres moved together, one to either side of the girl.

"Aniya," Taramis said. The naked girl reluctantly tore her gaze from the Sleeping God. "You," Taramis said, "are the first chosen, above your sisters, for your purity."

"This poor one is honored greatly," the girl whispered.

"At your birth were you sealed to the Sleeping God. Do you now willingly serve him?" Taramis knew the answer even before the light of ecstacy appeared in the girl's eyes. The cruel-eyed noblewoman had prepared both long and well.

"This poor one begs to serve," the girl replied, her voice soft yet eager.

The flutes now shrieked in frenzy.

"O great Dagoth," Taramis cried, "accept this, our offering and pledge to thee. Accept thy first anointing, against the Night of thy Return."

His face still a portrait of gentleness, Xanteres'

clawed fingers gripped Aniya's hair, bent her forward over the head of the alabaster form, then bent back her head so that her neck was a tight curve of smooth skin. From within his robes he produced a dagger with a gilded blade, and the gilded steel bit smoothly into the smooth curve. A crimson fountain splashed over the god's face.

"O great Dagoth," Taramis shouted, "thy servants anoint thee!"

"O great Dagoth," the priests echoed, "thy servants anoint thee!"

Taramis sank to her knees, bowed her head to the marble. Wrapped in her own intentness, she was unaware of the rustle as the priests knelt and bowed as well. "O great Dagoth," she prayed, "thy servants await the Night of thy Coming! *I* await the Night of thy Coming."

The massed voices of the priests followed fervently on hers. "O great Dagoth, thy servants await the Night of thy Coming."

Aniya's body jerked one last time and was still where it had fallen, forgotten, her glazing eyes staring at the no longer spreading pool of her blood on the pale tiles.

XVI

Conan's horse picked its way along the stony valley floor, its rider wearing a stony expression. He kept his mind focused on the way before him, not allowing thoughts to stray.

"We must go on," Jehnna told him, and his face hardened more. "I know the way, and we must go on."

He waited until they topped a notch, its far slope leading into another valley, before speaking. "I can have you safe in Shadizar in two days. One, if we near kill the horses." From that rise he could see out of the mountains toward the rising sun, out onto the Zamoran plain. Two days, he thought, without pushing the animals too hard. No thoughts but how far the horses could travel, and how fast.

"It is my destiny!" she protested

"Your destiny is not to die in these moutains. I will return you to your aunt's palace."

"You cannot interfere with my destiny!"

"Erlik take your destiny," he growled.

She drew alongside of him. "What of Valeria?" she demanded. "Yes, I heard that, too. I know what reward my aunt promised you."

It was a titanic effort to keep his face free of emotion, but Conan did it. A debt to be repaid, no matter the cost. But cost to himself, not to Jehnna. "I can protect you as we travel, but not if we hunt danger. Or do you think this treasure will simply be lying about unguarded?"

"Valeria—"

"She'd not ask me to trade your life for hers," he snapped. "Now be quiet, and follow me."

For a time she was indeed silent, though sulking and muttering angrily under her breath. Occupied with his own troubles, Conan refused to acknowledge her anger

Abruptly she said, "It is there. I know it is, Conan. We must go there. Please!"

Despite a resolve not to, he looked where she was pointing. The gray-sloped mountain was not high, but near the base its stone flanks split unnaturally into hundreds of granite fingers and spires. A maze, he remembered Jehnna calling this journey. That was a maze in truth, where an army could lie in wait unseen until you were in their midst. It was no place to take a young girl, not in the Karpash

Mountains, not even if the treasure Taramis wanted was in there. They would circle to the south, he decided, giving that particular mountain a wide berth. He rode on in silence.

"Conan!"

He closed his ears, refused to hear.

"Conan!"

Suddenly it impinged on the Cimmerian's mind that it was not Jehnna's voice he heard. His hand went to the worn hilt of his broadsword. That the caller knew his name could mean much or little. Then, from where a fold of land had momentarily hidden it, a horse appeared, with a Corinthian military saddle and a wiry, dark-eyed rider.

A broad grin split Conan's face. "Malak!" he shouted "I feared you were dead."

"Not I!" the small thief roared back. "I am too handsome to die!"

On Malak's heels the others came, Bombatta and Zula, Akiro easing his seat in his saddle and complaining about his old bones. The black woman rode straight to Jehnna, and the two of them put their heads together for talk pitched not to travel to any ears but their own.

"What happened with the Corinthians?" Conan demanded. "And how did you find us?"

Akiro opened his mouth, but Malak rushed in. "When they saw you two topping the pass, about half the fools rode off shouting about being first to ride the girl. Don't you all glare at me! Mitra, they said it, not me! In any case, cutting the numbers down gave Akiro a chance to work. Tell them what you did, Akiro.''

Akiro opened his mouth again.

"He made a tiger appear," Malak laughed. "It was as big as an elephant! Fidesa witness my words! The horses went mad." He caught the old wizard's gaze on him, and subsided with a weak, "You tell the rest, Akiro."

"It was a small illusion," Akiro said. He did not take his eyes off Malak as he spoke, as if afraid that did he look away the wiry man would cut him off again. "Even with fewer of the Corinthians, I had no time for more. It was of sight and smell only, and could not even move, but the horses, to our great luck, did not know that. They did indeed go mad. Ours as well. But it enabled us to escape. Without the packhorse, as you see, but with our skins in one piece."

There was a deal too much of sorcery on this journey to suit Conan, but he could not complain when it saves his friends' lives. Instead he said, "It was fortuitous you found us. We entered these accursed mountains together, and it is well that we leave together."

Malak started to speak, then snapped his mouth firmly shut at Akiro's glare.

"Fortune had naught to do with it," the yellow-skinned mage said. "It was this." He held a leather cord with a small, carved stone dangling at its end. With a deft motion he set the stone to spinning in a circle, yet almost immediately the circle lengthened and narrowed until the stone swung back and forth in a line that pointed directly at Conan.

The Cimmerian drew a deep breath. Yet more sorcery! "I do not like such things asociated with me," he said, and was pleased that he had not yelled it.

"Not with you," Akiro assured him. "With the amulet. Such a thing is much less complex than a living person, and thus easier to fix on. Had I had some of your hair, or some garments you had worn, I could have found you much more quickly."

"Crom!" Conan breathed. His hair! He would never allow a sorcerer to have such, no matter how much a friend he seemed at the moment.

Akiro went on as if the Cimmerian had not spoken. "With only an inanimate object as a focus, the circle barely changed at first. It was very difficult to read a direction. Much like finding your way through a building in the dark, by feel."

"And Bombatta did not want to follow it," Malak burst out. "He said he didn't trust Akiro." His last words trailed off to a murmur, and he gave a worried look at Akiro.

"It is all right," Akiro said. "I was finished."

All the while they talked Bombatta had sat his horse, glaring from Conan to Jehnna and back again. Now he growled, "Did he harm you, child?"

Jehnna looked up, startled, from her conversation with Zula. "What? Why, what do you mean, Bombatta? Conan protects me, even as you do."

Her answer did not seem to satsify the black-armored man. His face darkened, and the scars on it became livid. He looked at Akiro, hesitated visibly, then spoke. "I must know, wizard. Is she still an innocent?"

"Bombatta!" Jehnna protested, and Zula spoke close behind her.

"That is no question to be asked, or answered," the black woman growled.

"Tell me true, wizard," Bombatta said insistently, "for our lives and more, much more than you can know, depend on it."

Akiro pursed his lips, then nodded slowly. "She is an innocent. I sense it so strongly, I wonder that the rest of you cannot." As Bombatta sagged with a relieved sigh, the round-bellied mage moved his horse closer to Conan's and lowered his voice. "It is a thing of the spirit and not of the flesh, as I said once before," he murmured.

Conan colored, and colored more when he realized that he had. "You pry," he muttered. "Do not use your wizardry on me."

"Use the vial I gave you," Akiro said. "Use it, and ride away from here. Take the girl, if you wish. I do not doubt you could persuade her to go with you. In another night or two." A faint leer touched his lips, and was gone. "There can be nothing in this for you, Cimmerian, save more wounds of the kind that neither show nor heal."

Conan scowled silently, denying the temptation to put his hand to his belt-pouch to see if the small stone vial was still there. Valeria, and a debt still unpaid. He became aware of Jehnna's voice.

"He says he will not take me, but I know it is there. I know!"

Bombatta turned a scowling visage to the Cimmerian. "Well, thief, do you abandon your precious Valeria? Did those Corinthians frighten your manhood from you? Or did you ever have—?"

Conan's eyes were so cold that the scar-faced warrior cut off his words. Bombatta's emotions were writ plain on his features, realization of what he had done, anger at having been afrighted even for a moment, rage that the others had seen it. He gripped his tulwar so hard that the hilt creaked, but the big Cimmerian made no move toward his own weapon.

Patience, Conan told himself. In the rugged mountain ranges of Cimmeria a man without patience was a man who was soon dead. There would be time for killing later. When he spoke his voice was icy calm.

"I would not take her where she wants to go without other eyes to watch, and more blades to guard her. We have them, now." He pulled his horse up beside Bombatta's. "Let us not delay, Zamoran. We must be back in Shadizar by tomorrow night, and we have matters to settle, you and I, when this is done."

"I will look forward to it," Bombatta snarled.

"And I," Conan said, starting forward again, "will look back upon it."

XVII

Half a day's riding it took to reach those broken fingers of stone, and they looked no better to Conan once he was in them than they had from a distance. Quickly the rough gray walls rose around them, and the way narrowed until they were forced to ride in single file. Hundreds of confined passages crossed and re-crossed like miniature canyons, with thick stone separating them. Sometimes half a score choices of direction were presented at once, and each was more cramped and crooked than the one before.

"To the right," Jehnna said from directly behind him. "The right, I said. No, not that one. That one over there! It's close, now. Oh, we could move twice as fast if you'd only let me lead."

"No!" Bombatta shouted.

Conan said nothing, reining in to study the possi-
bilities ahead, three narrow corridors through the
stone leading off in different directions. Very narrow corridors. It was not the first time Jehnna had
asked to lead the way, and he had long since tired
of explaining the dangers to her. Bombatta now
refused to leave her side because, he claimed, he
did not trust the Cimmerian not to allow her to go
ahead of him. After Bombatta's display at the
rejoining, Conan was sure the Zamoran simply did
not want to leave her alone with him, but the
problem before him left no time to worry about
that.

"Why have we stopped?" Jehnna demanded.
"That is the way. Right there." She pointed to the
center gap.

"It is too narrow for the horses," Conan said.
With some difficulty, for the gray walls were already close, he swung down from his saddle and
moved ahead of his horse. "We will have to leave
them."

He did not like doing it. Hobbled, they would
not wander far, but even a short distance could
make a difference in this. And without horses
there was no hope in Zandru's Nine Hells of reaching Shadizar in time. The others had dismounted
and were fastening hobbles between their mounts'
forelegs, or pushing past the animals to join him.

"Malak," he said, "best you stay with the
horses."

The small thief started and stared at the stone

around them with a sickly look. "Here? Sigyn's Bowl, Conan, I don't think we should divide ourselves. Keep our forces together, eh? A man can't even breath in here."

About to make a sharp retort, Conan stopped. He himself had been thinking much about how close the stone was, how it seemed almost to cut off the air. But he was not one to be affected by tight passages or close spaces. He studied the others' faces, trying to see if any of them felt what he did. Jehnna was all impatience, while Zula had the set face of one who expected combat at any moment. Bombatta glowered, as usual, and Akiro appeared thoughtful, also as usual. Perhaps it was all in his imagination. And perhaps not.

"Yes, we'll stay together," he said. He drew his sword in one hand, his dagger in the other. "Thus will I mark our way," with the dagger he scratched an arrow on the stone, pointing toward the horses, "that we can find the horses again. Stay close."

To Jehnna's eager urging Conan moved down the rough-walled passage, though not so quickly as she would have liked, and every ten paces he scratched another arrow on the stone. If the worst came, he thought, even Jehnna could find the animals with these. Even alone she might have a chance of escape.

At times they had to turn sideways, stone scraping their chests and backs, for some stretches were so strait not even Zula or Jehnna could walk through them normally. However Conan walked, he kept his sword advanced and his dagger ready for anything that managed to get past the longer blade. As he moved deeper into the maze, his sense of something ill grew. Almost could he put a name now to what seemed to permeate the stone through which they made their way. It was like the remembrance of a memory of the stench of death, so faint the nose could not smell it, so tenuous the mind could not grasp it, yet there to be touched by the most primitive instincts.

He looked back at the others, and this time found his unease mirrored on their faces, all save Jehnna's.

"Why do we move so slowly?" the slender girl demanded. Vainly, she tried to push past the big Cimmerian, but there was barely width enough for him to pass alone. "We are almost there."

"Akiro?" Conan said.

The gray-haired wizard's face was twisted as if he had a bad taste in his mouth. "I have sensed it since we entered these passages, but it grows stronger as we go. It is . . . a foulness." He stopped to spit. "But it is old, ancient, and I do not think it threatens us. We are more than a few centuries too late for that."

Conan nodded, and continued on, but he was not convinced. His own senses might not be magical, but they had kept him alive in many places where he could well have died, and they told him there was danger here. He kept a firm grip on his weapons

With startling suddenness the passage spilled out into a large open area. Here the rock had been cut away, and the stone remaining carved in intricate patterns to floor a great courtyard that fronted a temple hewn from the very side of the mountain. Massive fluted columns ran across the face of the temple, and once a score of obsidian statues, four times the height of a man, had stood between them. Now only one remained, an ebon warrior holding a tall spear, with the features of his face worn away by wind and rain. Of the others only shattered chunks of black stone and the stumps of their legs remained.

Conan sheathed his dagger and grabbed Jehnna's arm as she tried to run to the temple. "Take care, girl," he told her. "I'll risk much here, but you I risk as little as possible."

Bombatta seized her other arm, and the two men stared coldly at one another above her head. The promise of death was strong between them. It was another reason to wish the journey done, Conan thought. Such promises as that could not remain unfulfilled forever.

"Let me go," Jehnna said, twisting in their grasp. "I must find the Horn. It is inside there. Let me go!"

Zula, sneering at both men, put her hands on Jehnna's shoulders. "Will you tear her apart, then? Or perhaps crush her between you?"

Conan let his hand fall away, and Bombatta was only an instant behind. Zula drew the girl away, speaking softly in her ear. Conan met Bombatta's glare unblinkingly.

"This will be settled, thief," the scar-faced man said.

"In Shadizar," Conan said, and the other jerked a nod of agreement.

When Conan reached the temple, Akiro was attempting to trace with his finger weather-worn carving in the pedestal on which the obsidian statue stood. Little was left.

"What are you trying to do?" Malak laughed at the old wizard. "Read decorative carving? And to speak of it, I've seen better scrollwork done by a one-eyed drunkard."

Sighing, Akiro straightened and dusted his hands. "I could read it, in part at least, were it not so badly eroded. It is script, not scrollwork. This place is much older even than I believed. The last writings in this language were done more than three thousand years ago, and even then it was a dead tongue. Only scattered fragments remain. Perhaps I can find more inside."

"We are not here to decipher old languages," Bombatta growled.

Privately Conan agreed, but all he said was, "Let us get on with it, then."

Rock doves burst from their nests high behind the massive columns, their wingbeats like an explosion in the stillness, as Conan strode to the tall bronze doors, covered with the verdigris of centuries. Through the thick green could be seen a huge open eye, worked deeply into the metal of each door. A large bronze ring hung below each eye.

"We'll never get that open," Malak said, eyeing the corrosion.

Conan grasped one thick ring for an experimental heave. To his surprise the door swung out with a squeal of hinges long ungreased. It was but chance that it opened so, he told himself. If men used those doors, they would grease the hinges. He did not like the relief he felt at that. Still, he told himself, he was there to see to Jehnna's safety, not to flaunt his own bravery.

"Keep a sharp eye," he commanded, "and your guard up." Then he led the way inside.

Beyond the great doors the dust of centuries lay thick on the floor. Torches stood along the intricately carved walls in golden brackets, untarnished by the years but festooned in cobwebs. Above them the ceiling was lost in shadows, and the vast hall stretched before them into darkness.

Suddenly Zula screamed as a spider, its outstretched legs wide enough to cover a man's hand, ran across her bare foot.

"Only a spider," Malak said, crushing it beneath his foot. He kicked the pulped remains away. "No need to be afraid of a—" The wiry thief cut off with a yelp as Zula's staff whistled toward his face and halted, quivering, no more than a finger-width from his nose. His eyes crossed staring at it.

"I am not afraid," Zula hissed. "I simply do not like spiders." Rustlings sounded deeper in the hall, and she peered in that direction nervously. "And rats. I especially do not like rats."

Conan lifted a torch down from the wall and sheathed his sword to dig into his pouch for flint and steel. "If these still burn," he began.

Akiro's lips moved, and fire suddenly danced atop his bunched fingers. He touched it to the torch, which burst aflame with a crackle that was loud in the still hall. "It will burn," he said.

"Can you not wait until you are asked?" Conan said drily as he stuffed the lighting implements back. Akiro shrugged apologetically.

Bombatta and Malak lit torches from Conan's, and they started warily down the great hall. Their feet disturbed dust unmarked save for the small tracks of rats. The bones of small animals and birds lay scattered about, some buried in the dust, some atop it. Long had it been since anything had moved there save the rodents and their prey. The chittering of rats, held back by fire and the strange smell of humans, followed them, and the torches' flames were reflected in hundreds of tiny, hungry eyes. Zula muttered and swiveled her head as if trying to watch all ways at once. Malak no longer made fun of her discomfort; he rigidly avoided looking at those glittering eyes, and mixed curses and prayers to a score of gods in a low monotone.

At the far end of the hall were broad stone steps leading up to a dais atop which sat a high-back throne of marble. Before that throne lay a small pile of age-dried bones, and on its seat another pile with a human skull in its midst, empty, shadowed eye-sockets staring at Conan and his companions. Armor, garments, a crown, whatever that man had once worn, were all long gone to dust.

Jehnna pointed to their right, to a wide, arched doorway half-hidden in the darkness. "There," she said. "That is the way."

Conan found himself relieved that the treasure— the horn, had not Jehnna called it?—was not on that throne. Many years before he had taken the sword he carried from a throne not too different from this one, and it had not been an experience he would care to repeat.

Bombatta had moved to the archway as soon as the girl spoke, and thrust his torch through it. "Stairs!" he muttered. "How much deeper into the bowels of this place must we go?"

"As deep as we must," Conan said. And pushing Bombatta aside, he started down.

XVIII

The wide stairs spiraled down into the depths of the mountain, and here Conan could see signs of the earthquake that had toppled the statues in front of the temple. Cracks spider-webbed the walls, and once there was a jog in the stairs, as if someone had cut neatly through them then pushed one part a handspan to the side. True spiders had been there once, as well. Thick cobwebs clogged the passage, but at the touch of the Cimmerian's torch they hissed and flared and melted away.

"I do not like this, Conan," Malak whispered loudly. "Ogon strike me, but I don't."

"Then wait above," Conan replied.

"With the rats!" The small man's voice was a squeak, and Zula chuckled, though not strongly.

A final turn and the stairs led into a long chamber with a high vaulted ceiling supported by what seemed at first glance to be golden columns, a row of them along each wall. Nearly half the columns were toppled, though, their broken pieces littering the dusty, mosaicked floor, and the pieces showed thin hammered gold-leaf atop ordinary gray stone. The ceiling was worked in a profusion of strange symbols, only one of which Conan could even recognize. An open eye, as on the bronze doors, repeated over and over among the other designs. What it meant he could not begin to guess.

"Conan," Akiro called, "this seems the only way out other than the stairs."

The wizard stood at the far end of the chamber by a broad door that seemed of iron, yet had no spot of rust on it. It had no hinges either, Conan saw, as if it were merely a huge metal plate set in the stone.

"This is the way," Jehnna whispered eagerly. She stared intently at the door, or at something beyond. "We must go on."

The door's dark gray surface was smooth except for the inevitable open eye in its center and two snarling demons' heads near the bottom. Tusks, like those of a wild boar, curved out from the open mouths of those grotesque heads. If the door could not be pushed open, Conan thought, then possibly . . . He rapped his sword sharply against each of the grimacing demon heads. From one gaping mouth wriggled a scarlet centipede; its bite was sure, slow and agonized death. Malak leaped from its way as it scurried for a hiding place among the fallen columns.

Sheathing his sword, Conan handed his torch to Zula and squatted before the door. One hand he placed in each demon mouth. As he had thought, his hands fit easily. He heaved upward.

"Handles," Malak exclaimed.

With every muscle straining, Conan began to wonder if he had been right in reaching the same conclusion as the smaller man. The metal slab moved no more than if it were a part of the mountain. Suddenly Bombatta was there beside him, grasping one of the demon heads. Conan shifted both hands to the other, and redoubled his effort. Tendons stood out along his neck and thighs, and every sinew of him cried out. Silver flecks danced before his eyes. And the iron slab lurched up a handsbreadth. Slowly then, with a metallic racheting noise, the door rose, until Conan and Bombatta between them held it above their heads.

"In," Conan rasped. "Quickly."

The others of the party squeezed hurriedly by the two big men, then Bombatta released his hold and followed. Conan's thews quivered with the strain of holding the weighty door alone, yet he hesitated. When he released it, it would come down, and look as he might, he could see no demons' open mouths nor other means of lifting it from the other side. They would be trapped. But if he could not find a way to prop it open, he would *have* to let it fall.

Murmuring to himself thoughtfully, Akiro stepped to the wall beside the door, where a bronze rod ending in a large knob, embossed with the ever-present open eye, projected from the stone. The mage put a hand on the knob, pushed, and the rod sank into the wall.

Conan blinked. There seemed to be a lessening of the weight on him. He eased his upward pressure slightly. The door did not move. With a sour grunt he stepped from under it.

"I thank you," he told Akiro, "but now that I think of it, could you not have opened this yourself?"

"I could have," Akiro replied mildly, "but you said I should wait to be asked. As I was not—"

"Where are the others?" Conan cut him off.

The light of Akiro's torch lit one end of a narrow corridor, and there was no sign of anyone other than the two of them, nor any light from the other torches. Cursing, the Cimmerian set out down that hall at a run, with Akiro panting in his footsteps. The corridor opened into a large, circular chamber, and both men skidded to a halt in amazement. The others were already there, holding their torches high while they stared about them.

Directly opposite the door through which they entered a monstrous head of carved black stone, fanged and glaring, as tall as a big man, projected from the wall. Two other doorways, set equidistant around the circle from the first, led from the chamber. Or rather, one did, for the other was broken and choked with rubble that spilled in a fan into the room. The rest of the walls were carved in bas-relief, images of fabled beasts, gilded, with gems set for their eyes while others formed hooves and claws and horns. At intervals around the walls great plaques of gold were set, covered with strange script. The low domed ceiling was tied with onyx and set with diamonds and sapphires, twinkling in the light of the torches, as if to represent a night sky.

Akiro rushed to one of the golden plaques and ran his fingers over the deep-carved script as if he did not believe his eyes. "This is the same language as outside, and more of it than exists in one place anywhere else in the world. I can . . . yes, I can make it out. Listen." He spoke on slowly, pausing to trace letters. "And on the thirteenth day of the Last Battle, the gods did come to war, and the mountains did tremble at their footsteps."

The rotund wizard went on, but Conan was more interested in what Jehnna was doing under Bombatta's watchful eye. She alone had not goggled at the riches of the chamber. Her eyes were only for the massive, terrible head of black stone. Now she stood before it, looking nowhere else. Beneath her feet was a circle of runes carved in the marble of the floor, and woven among them was a five-pointed star with straight lines joining its points.

Conan's breath caught in his throat. He knew the symbol of the star of old, knew it to his regret. A pentagram, a focus of sorcerous powers. He half-raised a hand to stop her. But there was Valeria. And Jehnna said this was her destiny, that she had been born to do this thing. The hand he had raised clenched into a fist until his knuckles cracked. He could do nothing else but see it through to the end.

From beneath her robes Jehnna produced the black velvet bag in which she carried the Heart of Ahriman. As the blood-red gem slipped into her palm its sanguine glow filled the chamber, and the jewels set in the ceiling seemed to glitter more fiercely. Carefully she set the Heart down before her in the pentagram; there was a small niche carved into which it fit exactly. As she straightened awareness faded from her eyes. In a trance, she chanted, and her words rang round the walls.

As she intoned the words, the radiance of the Heart increased, yet now it was focused, shining only on the great stone head, bathing it in crimson light. The black stone eyes especially seemed to reflect its glow, and crimson shadows danced in their depths, depths that had not been there moments before.

"It lives," Zula hissed, and Malak began muttering prayers.

"You must stop her," Akiro said suddenly, urgency riddling his voice. "Quickly, Conan, you must—" He broke off with a moan of denial that seemed wrung from his bones.

Soundlessly the stone jaws of the monstrous head opened, spreading wide enough to swallow three men whole, and in that mouth burned fire such as no eye there had ever before seen. Blood turned to flame, it was, and Conan found himself stepping back, a hand before to his face to shield him from heat that seemed to sear the very air. Though it pained his eyes to look, the Cimmerian saw a crystal spire in the midst of those flames. It was a pellucid column such as the one on which the Heart of Ahriman had rested in Amon-Rama's place, but atop this one was a horn of gold, like the horn of a bull. Neither spire nor horn seemed touched by the fiery tempest that roared about them.

Jehnna still stared as if not at this world, but worlds beyond. Her large eyes were blank, and her face lacked all expression. Slowly her hands rose to her shoulders, and her robes fell to her feet. Naked, she stood, slender curves bathed with the light of the flames before her, the birthmark between her small breasts glowing like those fires. With quick, unhesitating steps, she moved forward. Not a muscle moving, Bombatta watched her, and the light in his dark eyes could have been a reflection of the fiery furnace.

"No!" Conan shouted, yet even as he did it was too late.

Into the roaring flames Jehnna stepped. About her the fire flared as if in fury at her invasion, licking at her slim nudity, yet she moved deeper, unaware and unharmed. In both hands she lifted the golden horn, and with it walked from the blazing furnace, back to the pentagram.

For a moment she stood there, and all in the room seemed frozen where they stood. Then she sighed, sagged, and would have fallen had not Zula rushed to support her. Quickly the black woman pulled the girl's robes up about her.

"It is done," Bombatta said softly. "The Horn is in the hands of the One."

"Conan," Akiro said shakily, "there is something you must know."

Abruptly there was a wind in the chamber, an icy gale of eerie howls that they felt to their bones, yet which did not so much as bend the flames of the torches. Then it was gone as suddenly as it had come, and the fires in that huge mouth were gone, as well, but the chill of the wind remained.

"Conan," Akiro said again.

"Later," Conan snapped. One too many pieces of sorcery had he seen for a single day, and this last had come at no one's bidding that he could tell. "We leave *now!*" And barely waiting for Jehnna to gather the Heart of Ahriman, he hurried them from the chamber.

XIX

It was a procession that Conan led back along the narrow corridor, and he did not care for the feeling of it. Jehnna carried the golden horn hugged tightly to her bosom, and Bombatta and Zula hovered protectively on either side of her, interspersing solicitous looks for the slender girl with cold stares at each other. Though glad beyond measure that she was unharmed, the Cimmerian was troubled by what Jehnna had experienced, and troubled as well by the artifact she carried so carefully.

Akiro tugged at Conan's elbow. "I must talk with you," he said quietly, glancing back at Bombatta. "In private. It is urgent."

"Yes," Conan agreed distractedly. He had come in contact with sorcery many times before in his young life, many more than he wished to remember.

Betimes he found he could sense it, and what he sensed from the golden object the girl clutched to her breast was the odor of evil. Very much he wanted to be gone from that place, to be back in Shadizar with the thing done. "In private, Akiro," he murmured. "Later."

Malak ran before them, dancing in his eagerness to leave. "Hurry!" he called over his shoulder. "This place is ill! Mitra's Bones! Hurry!" He darted from view ahead, and his words faded away.

"Fool," Conan muttered. "This is no time to be separated." Then he was into the chamber of gilded columns, and he fell silent as well.

Malak was there, rolling his eyes nervously. Also there were more than a score of warriors in black leather armor of archaic design, leaning on long spears. The smallest of the men was head and shoulders taller than Conan or Bombatta. They were as black as the obsidian statue before the temple, and Conan was relieved to see their chests rise and fall with breathing. They were men, not statues come to life. That had been his first thought.

Two of the warriors stepped forward. One had a crest of long white hair spilling down the back of his bronze helmet; the other wore no helmet, but rather a black leather skull-cap from which hung long fringes of red hair. He with the white crest spoke. To Jehnna.

"Long have we waited for you, for the One. We have slept, as our god sleeps, and we have awaited the day of your coming. The Night of Awakening approaches.''

Bombatta shifted uneasily, and Akiro's breath whistled between his teeth.

"This girl has no part in your ways," Conan said. "We crave pardon if we have disturbed your temple, but we have far to travel, and we must go."

All the while he noted the disposition of the ebon warriors. He had no wish to fight if it could be avoided, but these men seemed to be saying that this was their temple, for all it looked not to have known a human tread in centuries. And men often grew violent when they thought strangers interfered with their religion.

"You may go," the towering black warrior replied. "For bringing us the girl, the One, your lives are given to you. But she remains with us."

Making every attempt to seem casual, Conan stepped between the tall warrior and Jehnna. "She is not the One you seek," he said, but the ebon man ignored him and spoke again to Jehnna.

"For all the years we have slept, guarding the Horn of Dagoth, waiting for you, for the One who could touch the Horn. Now will the Sleeping God be awakened, and his vengeance will spread against those who betrayed—''

Conan caught a flicker of motion out of the corner of his eye as Bombatta's arm whipped forward, and a dagger blossomed in the tall man's throat. Blood poured from the black giant's mouth as he fell, and pandemonium broke loose in the chamber.

"Back!" Conan shouted. There was no way forward except through huge men who were raising their spears and snarling with fury. "Back! Quickly!" The Cimmerian thrust his torch into one tall warrior's face, beat aside another's spear thrust, and ran a third through the middle.

A metallic racheting caught his ear. Sword dancing desperately to hold off an ever-increasing number of spears, he risked a quick glance over his shoulder. The great iron door was descending in jerks, and it did not have far to fall. With a roar he attacked, his blade a grim blur of razor steel before him, the sheer fury of him forcing his opponents back despite their greater numbers. With a suddenness that caught them all off-guard, he whirled and threw himself into a rolling dive toward the rapidly closing doorway. The bottom of the iron door scraped his shoulder, then he was through, and the slab settled against the floor with a heavy, grating thud.

Akiro, Malak and Zula stared down at him worriedly, but there was no time for their worry. "We must hurry," he said as he scrambled to his feet. " 'Tis likely they got a spear point or two under the edge of that trying to stab me, and if so they'll lever it up soon enough."

"I will see what I can do about that," Akiro said. Delving in his pouch, he drew out materials and began drawing symbols on the metal of the door.

"You could have given me a little warning," Conan muttered to Malak. "A shout that you were letting the door fall."

"Bombatta caught us all by surprise," Malak replied. "He grabbed Jehnna and darted in here before any of the rest of us could move. I guess he pulled that rod out as soon as he was past the door."

"There," Akiro said, stepping back from his labors. A string of faintly glowing symbols, each of which resisted efforts to focus the eye on it, stretched across the door from side to side. "That should hold them for a time."

Conan found he was no longer interested in whether the door held or not. "Where *is* Jehnna?" he demanded. "And Bombatta?"

Zula spun to stare down the dark hall. "I was so worried about you," she whispered, "that I did not. . . . If he has hurt her. . . ."

Conan did not wait to hear the rest. He sped toward the chamber of the great stone head as fast as his legs would carry him. It was empty. Without hesitation he took the one way out other than the way he had come, the unblocked, third corridor.

Grim thoughts filled the Cimmerian's head. Perhaps Bombatta meant to try spiriting Jehnna back to Shadizar without him, to cheat him of his reward. It would be like the Zamoran, he thought, to rob Valeria of a chance at rebirth just to strike at him.

There would be no waiting until Shadizar now. The time for accounting had come.

The corridor ran straight as an arrow, without bend or fork, without a doorway leading to another chamber. Like a tunnel, the corridor had been carved from the living rock of the mountain, its walls, ceiling and floor polished as smooth as marble. Dust dulled and covered all, now, and it was in that dust that the light of his torch showed the traces of those he followed, signs as plain to his keen eyes as ruts in a wagon road. The spaces between the tracks told him they, too, were running.

Suddenly the hallway spilled into a large, square chamber filled with thick, fluted columns set close together and supporting a ceiling lined with cracks and fissures. Many of the columns were filled with cracks as well, some seeming to need only a breath to topple. Dust-covered implements lay among them, fallen braziers with high, tripod legs, things that might have been tall stands to hold torches, others the purposes of which he could not guess.

Conan's torch was enough for him to make another door ahead, a deeper black rectangle in the shadows. The tracks in the dust led toward that door as well, but he stopped his headlong dash. Bombatta could be hidden anywhere among those myriad columns, and tracks so plain could lead to an ambush. In a cautious crouch, poised to spring in any direction, broadsword at the ready, the big Cimmerian advanced. His eyes probed the dark about him for the slightest hint of movement.

"Jehnna," he called softly, then louder, "Jehnna!" The name echoed, and he shouted over it, louder still, "Jehnna!"

Then he saw Bombatta, standing beside the far doorway with a thick rod of rusted iron, a good three paces long, in his hands. The Zamoran moved quickly for such a big man. He thrust the rod crossways between two cracked pillars like a lever and heaved.

Time seemed to slow for Conan as the columns bowed outwards in opposite directions, began to fall in chunks. The ceiling above him groaned; bits of stone and dirt pelted him.

In one smooth motion the Cimmerian turned and threw himself back the way he had come, away from collapsing stone. The roar of falling rock reverberated through the chamber. Something struck Conan's head, and darkness swallowed him.

Jehnna crouched where Bombatta had left her, peering down the corridor down which they had fled. He had fled, she thought angrily. She had been dragged behind him like a bundle. Until reaching this spot he had refused to listen to her pleas that he help the others, then he told her to wait and dashed back. It was all very well that he put her safety first, but he should have listened to her sooner. Golden-red sunlight shone through a crack at the top of a huge stone slab behind her, but she did not look at it. Daylight and the way back to Shadizar lay on the other side of that thick slab, but Conan was still behind her, in the depths of the mountain. What if he were injured, and needed her? What if. . . .

Running footsteps announced Bombatta's return. He scrambled up the slope of the corridor in haste.

"Is he unharmed?" she demanded

Dust and dirt covered the scar-faced man, and blood trickled from a scratch on his cheek. He started past her, then stopped suddenly, his face paling. "Where's the horn, child?" he demanded. "Zandru's Nine Hells, if you've lost it. . . ."

"It is here." She showed him the bundle she had made, wrapped in strips torn from her cloak. It was her destiny, she knew, this quest for the Horn of Dagoth, but there was something about the golden object that made her want not to touch it. The Heart of Ahriman and the Horn of Dagoth were together, swathed in layers of white wool, and she truly wished there were more layers. Many more. "Where is . . . where are the others?"

"Dead," Bombatta replied curtly. Huge muscles straining, he threw his weight against the massive slab of stone.

Jehnna sat as if poleaxed. Dead? Conan could not be dead. She could not imagine him as dead. Or the others, she told herself quickly. Zula, Akiro, even Malak, had taken on special meaning to her. She did not want to think of any of them being harmed. But the tall youth with the strange sapphire eyes and the hands that were so gentle when they did not hold a sword, he was more than special. "I cannot believe it," she whispered. The great slab fell outwards with a crash, raising a cloud of dust and letting in a flood of fading sunlight. "I heard him call my name. I know that I did."

"Come, Jehnna. We have little time, child."

Bombatta seized her wrist in his huge hand, pulling her after him through the opening. They were on the very edge of the large courtyard before the temple. The sun sat crimson on the mountaintops to the west. With a wary eye on the tall bronze temple doors and cursing under his breath, Bombatta hurried her into the maze of high stone fingers and spires.

"I will not believe Conan is dead," she told him.

"One of the marks," the black-armored man said, pointing to an arrow scratched in the rock. "Now to find the horses. We can cover leagues before full dark."

"Bombatta, I will not believe it. Did you see him fall?"

"I saw," Bombatta said harshly. He did not slow his pace, and his iron grip on her wrist made certain she kept up. "He was running, like the thief and dog that he was, and the black warriors cut him down. Him, and the others, as well. I had to pull down the ceiling to block them off from us. Ah, the horses."

The hobbled animals were still bunched together. Jehnna could not have told whether they had wandered from where they were left even had she thought of it, and her mind was on other matters.

"Perhaps he was only wounded," she began, then cut off at the strange look Bombatta was giving her. His eyes burned with intensity.

"We could go anywhere," he said softly. "We could go to Aghrapur. A Turanian wizard, or even King Yildiz himself, would give enough for those things you carry to keep us in luxury for the rest of our lives." Abruptly he lifted her onto a saddle. "Guard them well, Jehnna," he said, and began loosing the horses' hobbles. He tied the reins of each horse he freed to those of the next, and when he mounted he had the other four animals on a long lead.

"What are you doing?" she demanded. "We cannot take those."

"We will need them," Bombatta said. "It is a long way to Aghrapur."

"We go to Shadizar, not Aghrapur. And I will not leave the others without horses so long as there is any chance one of them remains alive. If you wish to take the horses, then you must take me back into the temple and show me their bodies."

Bombatta shook his head. "It is too dangerous for you."

"Dangerous or not," she insisted, "I will not leave him so."

The fury that clouded the massive warrior's face made her want to cower. It took all of her will to keep her back straight, to look him in the eye with outward calm.

Dropping the reins of the other horses, he moved his own closer to hers. "Him! Him, and again him! We could have gone anywhere." Every word came from him like a piece of iron. "Anywhere, child." Abruptly his scarred visage twisted in pain. Jehnna stared; she had never before seen Bombatta show pain. The agonized grimace lasted but a moment, then his face was normal again, save that in going from his eyes the burning seemed to have left them dull and flat. "We go to Shadizar," he said hoarsely and, taking the reins from her hands, began to lead her through the maze.

Jehnna clutched the bundle, containing all she had come so far to find, tightly against her breast, and would not allow herself to look back. Conan or her destiny. One at the cost of the other. She wondered how there could be such pain. How could the gods allow it? Slumping, no longer able to find the strength to sit straight, she wept softly and let herself be led.

XX

Through thick clouds of smothering darkness Conan clawed his way back to consciousness and scrambled to his feet with sword in hand. Akiro and Zula stared at him in amazement. Malak tossed a fist-sized rock into the shadows between the columns and dusted his hands.

"About time you were awake," the small thief said. "By Mehen's Scales, I was beginning to think you were going to sleep until we were all dead."

"How long?" Conan said. He felt the side of his head. It was tender, and a fan of dried blood descended from his hair

Malak shrugged, but Akiro said, "Perhaps two turns of the glass, perhaps a little longer. It is difficult to tell exactly. We found you lying like a stunned ox. I did what I could, but it is best with head injuries to let wakefulness come naturally.''

"I have a few herbs that help blows to the head," Zula said, "but there is no water to steep them in.''

The Cimmerian nodded, and immediately wished he had not as the chamber seemed to spin around. Desperately he fought off the dizziness. He could allow no weakness now.

The far end of the dim chamber was now a mass of stone, fragments of fluted columns mixed with chunks of the mountain above in sizes from that Malak had held to boulders larger than a man. Three of the rusted metal stands Conan had thought made to hold torches had been set upright. Their torches burned atop them, casting a pale yellow pool about the four, a pool that quickly faded into shadows among the columns. Not all the light came from the torches, however. From down the unblocked passage came a flickering azure glow that was painful to the eye.

"What is that blue light?'' Conan asked

"A ward,'' Akiro told him. "I managed to lay nine sets before those tall fellows got the door open. Then I had to trigger the first and could lay no more. It is dangerous to place one of those while another burns close by.''

"How long,'' Conan began, and got his answer before he could complete the question.

The azure flickering increased in speed, and Akiro bent to draw symbols in the dust with a finger and mouth his silent incantations. With a last flash of brilliant blue the light was gone. In an instant it began again, and a shriek echoed down the corridor as it did.

Akiro tilted his head as if listening, then sighed. "One was very fast, but not their wizard, worse luck. If Bombatta had to slay one of them, he could as well have killed the one with the red crest. He is their mage, and without him they would never even have gotten that door open, much less reached my wards. And I must fight him with little more than my bare hands."

"I do not see why he had to kill any of them," Zula said angrily. "They offered no violence toward us, only speaking to. . . ." Her words trailed off with a sympathetic look at Conan, but he ignored it.

"I doubt they would have let us go without a fight," he said. "Not with Jehnna. In any case, I'll not let them spear me like a wild pig just because Bombatta started it."

"That's it," Malak said. "Ogon's Toenails, if a man attacks you, you carve him, and if it's all a mistake you can burn a little incense in the temples for his spirit."

"Not always the best way," Akiro said drily. "But those men are foul."

"I saw no foulness in them," Zula protested, and the wizard snorted.

"That is because you are not a mage, nor did you read the plaques, as I did. The unease we felt as we entered was put there by those men, and by those who came before them, over centuries. Human sacrifice was the least of it. They make the shamans you res—ah, assisted me with, seem as babes at play.''

"I care not if they're cannibals," Conan said. "It is past time for us to be getting out of here. Bombatta and Jehnna get closer to Shadizar with every moment, and I do not doubt he'll do his best to leave us out of what has happened when he tells Taramis of it. I do not intend to be cheated of my promised reward.''

Akiro looked at him pityingly, and Zula gaped. "But I thought . . . we thought . . . Jehnna. . . .'' She gestured helplessly at the jumbled stone filling the other end of the chamber.

"Bombatta pulled that down," Conan said. "He could not wait to face me in Shadizar. But I cannot think he pulled it down on his own head, nor on Jehnna's. We will dig our way out, and follow. There is but a night and a day left before we must be back in Shadizar.''

"You intend to dig through the mountain?" Malak said incredulously. The other two looked at the Cimmerian as if he had gone mad.

"I saw this chamber when it was whole," Conan told them as he strode to the mass of rock. "I know how much of it is gone." He seized a torso-sized piece of a column and heaved it loose; smaller stones slid free and bounced around his feet. "The passage Bombatta followed is no more than three or four paces from us. And we have only to clear a way wide enough to squeeze through." He carried the stone well into the columns before dropping it. There was room there for all they had to move and more. When he returned, the others remained where they had been, still staring at him. "Well?" he demanded. "Would you rather die here?" Without a word Zula came to dig at the stone.

Malak came more slowly, and not without a look over his shoulder at the old wizard. "Aren't you going to help, Akiro? You could wave your arms, and make all this disappear."

"You display your ignorance openly," Akiro snorted. "In any case, I must watch to trigger the next ward when this one fails. Unless you want your first warning of those spearmen to be when one spits you like a lamb."

"You trigger all of them now, old man. Then you could help."

The gray-haired wizard laughed derisively. "Do I teach you how to steal, my small thief? Be about something you know how to do."

Conan labored like an automaton, fixing his mind on the goal of freedom, refusing to allow the immensity of the task to daunt him. Two stones he moved for every one moved by Zula and Malak together. Sweat oiled him till he glistened in the torchlight, and there was always more sweat to wash away the dust. When, with a loud rumble, rock cascaded from above to replace all they had done, he chivied the others back to work without ceasing himself. He must reach Jehnna. He must repay his debt to Valeria. Jehnna. Valeria. The two swirled in his mind till he could not tell which drove him most.

When another ward failed and Akiro chanted to replace it, Malak stopped to watch, knuckling the small of his back. "You really read those plaques, Akiro?" he asked.

"Work,". Conan said, and after one glance at the Cimmerian's grim face Malak bent back to the stones.

Akiro, however, seemed to want to talk. He settled himself against a column and began. "Yes, I read them. Enough of them, at least. The golden horn that. . . ." He frowned at Conan, then went on. "It is the Horn of Dagoth."

"The black warrior called it that," Malak panted.

"Do not interrupt," the wizard replied acerbically. ";Millennia ago there was a war between the gods, which was not a rare thing in those times. In a great battle Dagoth was defeated by having the Horn ripped from his head and carried far away. The Horn carried what might be called his life-force, and without it he slowly turned to stone. According to the plaques, he sleeps, and when the Horn is placed again on his head he will wake."

"So that is why Taramis wants it," Conan said, still laboring. "To wake a god. Surely a god could bring Valeria back to life."

"Yes," Akiro sighed, "I suppose Dagoth could restore her to the living."

"So Taramis did not lie," Conan said with satisfaction.

As if he had received rest and cool water the Cimmerian increased his efforts. As the others slowed, he carried stones with greater speed. Zula fell trying to keep up with him, and could not stand. Conan paused to carry her back to Akiro, then rushed back to his labor. Later, when Malak dropped, the Cimmerian merely dragged him clear of the path he must follow from the stony blockage to where he threw the rocks.

He knew vaguely that they had dug past the end of the chamber, into the corridor, and still rock was piled before him. He knew it in a dim recess of his mind, but to acknowledge it might be the beginning of defeat, and he suppressed it ruthlessly without even being aware that he did so. Time lost all meaning to him. Effort lost all meaning. As if he were himself made of stone, incapable of tiring, he attacked the barrier relentlessly. Twin images drew him on. Valeria. Jehnna. He would not stop while life remained.

He tugged at a stone jammed into the tangle, tugged harder. It came free, and as it did the wall of rocks fell toward him. He stumbled back, cursing, barely avoiding being buried to the waist. Starting to turn away with the stone, he stopped abruptly with the realization that he had been looking over piled stone at a pale spot of light in the distance. He looked again, just to be sure he was not imagining it. The glow was still there. Letting the stone he had fall, he moved back to the chamber of columns.

Akiro sat cross-legged, staring gravely at the azure light from the corridor. Zula barely looked up, but Malak said tiredly from where he lay, "So you're finished, too, eh, Cimmerian? Well, we gave it a good try. Erlik take us, if we didn't."

"I am through," Conan said. "There is light. Sunlight, maybe." Malak made a strange sound, and quivered. It took Conan a moment to realize the small thief was laughing.

"We made it," Malak wheezed. "By Zandru's Darkest Hell and Mitra's Bones, they cannot stop us, Cimmerian."

"You are certain, Conan?" Akiro said worriedly.

"It could be torches in another chamber," Conan replied, "but there would have to be scores of them. The passage slopes upward. It must break ground." Or it could rise into the mountain, he thought, but would not say it. The light could be from sorcery or Zandru's Seventh Hell, but he needed to reach the surface above, and he would not admit it could be anything else.

"We must hope for sunlight," Akiro said finally. "The seventh ward yet holds, though not for much longer, and two more wait. You must get Zula and Malak out of here as quickly as possible. I will follow as soon as I can." He scurried back to his post at the mouth of the corridor. "Go man, or you may yet kill us all."

Conan helped Zula to her feet, and turned to

find Malak already wavering erect. The black woman tried to walk on her own, too, but the big Cimmerian found himself helping the pair to scramble over the last mound of stones and stagger upward toward the light. That glow seemed to have a restorative quality, for by the time Akiro caught up to them, both Zula and Malak were climbing without support and making good speed.

Even so, the old wizard called out, "Hurry! Hurry!" And there was that in his voice that made them move even faster.

The corridor ended in a rectangular opening, and the four stumbled out into the temple courtyard and the light of a sun not-yet fully risen in the east. Malak and Zula stared at it as if they had not believed they would ever see a sunrise again.

Conan had eyes only for the temple, with its huge columns and fallen statues. Unless the tall warriors were fools, he thought, there would be sentries. Yet as he hastened them all across the carven stones of the courtyard nothing moved from the temple save rock doves, flapping out from their nests high behind the columns. Then he realized there was no need to put sentries above when all of your enemies were trapped like rats beneath the mountain.

In the maze the thirsty whickering of the horses drew them quickly to the animals. Conan noted the missing hobbles and the tied reins, then the four of them were hurrying for the waterskins. Despite a throat that felt like gravel Conan first poured water into his horse's mouth. When it was his turn he tipped back his head and drank until forced to breath, let the water splash over his face while he gulped air, then drank more. He finished by giving his horse another drink. The animal would have more need to be refreshed than he, for he intended to ride it hard.

Suddenly the ground quivered beneath their feet. Conan grabbed the reins, but before he could soothe his mount another tremor shook the earth, followed by a rumbling boom from the direction of the temple.

Malak, clinging to a trembling horse, muttered, "What in the Nine-Fold Names of Khepra was that?"

Akiro coughed smugly. "I changed the incantation slightly. When they broke through the seventh ward, the last two were triggered together. Those spearman will not wake from this sleep, nor rise from this tomb to slaughter innocents for Dagoth." He smiled suddenly at Malak. "Do you see now why I could not invoke all the wards at once?"

" 'Tis good they will not trouble us further," Conan said, climbing into his saddle, "but we must ride if we are to reach Shadizar by the ceremony tonight. I will not let Bombatta cheat me of Valeria's life."

The smile disappeared from Akiro's face. "I did not tell you, Conan, when I thought we would die, for a man should not be burdened at his death with matters he cannot change. In truth, even now I fear it is too late. I tried to stop it when it could have been stopped, before she entered the furnace, but I was too slow."

"You babble, Akiro," Conan growled. "Speak what is on your mind, or let me ride for Shadizar."

"It was all on the plaques," Akiro said. "The Rite of Awakening takes three nights, and on each night a girl is sacrificed. On the Third Night, the sacrifice is the One who Bears the Horn, the innocent. It will be Jehnna."

"Perhaps it is not her," Zula said pleadingly. "Not even Bombatta would take her back to that."

"Bombatta called her the One," the old wizard sighed. "He knows she is to die."

Conan touched the dragon amulet on his chest. Pain filled him, and he wanted to howl it aloud as he had never given voice to pain before. Valeria. "Jehnna will not die," he said through clenched teeth.

"I like the girl, too," Malak protested, ignoring Zula's glare, "but, Badb's Holy Buttocks, we're all exhausted, and we could not reach Shadizar before nightfall if we killed the horses trying."

"Then when my horse dies," Conan replied grimly, "I will run, then crawl. But before all the gods I vow, Jehnna will survive this night if I must die for it." Without waiting to see if the others followed, he kicked his horse into motion, into a race with the rising sun.

XXI

From a balcony Taramis looked down on the marble-tiled courtyard where rested the Sleeping God, a canopy of fringed golden silk raised to shield him from the blazing sun. In a circle about the canopy, unprotected and perspiring, knelt half a score of priests in their robes and crowns of gold, chanting their prayers. Since the First Anointing there had continually been a circle of priests offering their devotions to Dagoth, with only a pause the night before for the Second Anointing.

Taramis ran her eyes over the other balconies overlooking this court, yet she knew there would be no one there to observe who should not see. For three days this part of her palace had been all but sealed from the rest. No slave or servant would come near to it without her express command, even if guards had not been posted with orders to slay any who tried. It was not that that cut at her like a whip's lash. She knew very well what it was that truly preyed on her mind, what it was she did not want to think about.

Hesitantly she looked at the sun, then jerked her gaze away. Already that distended yellow ball was past the zenith. *Well* past the zenith. And tonight came a configuration of the stars that would not come again for a thousand years. If Bombatta did not bring the girl in the next few hours, if the girl did not have what she had been sent for. . . . Taramis bit at her lip, heedless of the blood that came. It could not be so. It would not be so. She refused to die knowing that power and immortality would come to someone else a thousand years hence.

A deferential cough made her whirl, ready to flay whomever had dared to disturb her.

Xanteres stood in the doorway, his face as deceptively gentle as ever, but a gleam of exultation in his dark eyes. "She is come," he said grandly. "Bombatta has brought her."

Taramis abandoned dignity. She pushed past the white-bearded high priest and ran, speeding down corridors and stairs till she came to the great alabaster-columned entry hall of the palace, with its high, vaulted ceiling. And there, dusty, bedraggled and travel-stained, stood Bombatta, with his helmet under his arm, and Jehnna, clutching a dusty bundle, barely recognizable as once-white wool, to her bosom. Taramis hardly even noticed the massive black-armored warrior. Her eyes were all for the girl.

"Do you have it?" she whispered, approaching slowly. "By all that is sacred and holy, child, do you have it?"

Hesitantly, Jehnna held out the bundle she had clasped to her breasts. She swayed, and Taramis saw that she was exhausted. But the time for rest was not yet. Other, more important matters came first.

The tall Zamoran noblewoman looked around frantically for the high priest, ready to shout for him, but he was there. Reverently Xanteres held forward an elaborate golden casket within which were crystal supports wrought with all of Taramis' sorcerous skill and cunning.

"Place them there, child," Taramis said.

From the bundle Jehnna produced the Heart of Ahriman, sanguinely glowing, and placed it in the casket. Taramis held her breath. The dirty white wool dropped to the marble floor, and Jehnna was cradling the golden Horn of Dagoth in her hands.

As that, too, was laid on crystal supports within the casket, Taramis' hand twitched with the desire to touch it. Not yet, she reminded herself. Now it was death for any hand but Jehnna's. Later it would be hers alone to know.

With great reluctance Taramis closed the golden casket. "Take it," she commanded the high priest. "Guard it with your life." Xanteres bowed himself from her presence, and she turned her attention back to Jehnna and Bombatta. The girl swayed again. "Where are the bath girls?" Taramis demanded. "Must I have the fool wenches flayed?"

Two white-robed young women, black hair pinned in curls close to their heads, sped into the hall and fell to their knees before Taramis.

"The Lady Jehnna is travel weary," the beauteous princess told them. "She must be bathed and massaged. She must be properly garbed."

Jehnna smiled warmly, if tiredly, at the woman as they hurried to her. "It is so good to see you again," she said. "It seems years since I have had a proper bath. But where are Aniya and Lyella?"

The white-robed women's faces went blank, and Taramis hastened to fill the silence. "They are ill, child. You will see them later. Take her away! Can you not see she is near collapse?" She watched them lead Jehnna from the hall, then turned smiling to Bombatta. "It is done, then," she sighed.

"It is done," he said, but something in his eyes made her frown.

Her mind raced, searching for what could possibly be left yet undone. "The thief?" she said. "He is dead?"

"He is dead," Bombatta replied.

"You put your sword through him."

"No, but—"

Her hand flashed out, cracked against his face. "When the One holds the Horn," she quoted, "the sky-eyed thief must die. An he lives, danger comes on his shoulder and death rides his right hand.'' She drew a deep breath. ''You *know* what is written in the scrolls.''

''He lies entombed with half a mountain atop him,'' Bombatta growled sullenly.

''Fool! If you did not handle his corpse. . . . I will not take a chance, Bombatta, not even a small chance, not now. It is all too close to fruition. Treble the guard.''

''For one thief who is certainly dead?'' he barked.

''Do it!'' she commanded coldly. ''Let not so much as a mouse pass the palace walls without a spear in it.'' Not waiting for his reply she turned away. The Horn was at last in her possession, and if she could not touch it, she could at least gaze upon it. She had to gaze upon it.

The city of Shadizar was called 'the Wicked,' and what the eyes of its citizens had not seen had never happened under the heavens, yet the crowds in the streets gave wide passage to the four who rode into the city as dusk drew near. Weary and lathered were their horses, and the four—one a woman—seemed no less travel-worn, yet there was a grimness in their eyes, most especially in the strange blue eyes of the young giant who led them, that made even City Guardsmen decide to look elsewhere for evildoers and bribes.

Conan knew where a stable stood not far from Taramis' palace, and the horses were no sooner turned over to a hostler than he hurried into the streets.

Akiro caught up to him with an effort. "Slow down, my young friend. You must have a plan." Malak and Zula joined them, and the look of the four was enough to gain them as clear a path as when they had ridden.

"There is no time for slowing," Conan growled. "Or have you not looked at the sun?"

Ahead of them Taramis' palace came in view. The tall, iron-bound gates were closed, and six guards stood before them with slanted spears. On the walls more guards were appearing every moment, until they stood two paces apart all the way around the palace.

The wizard pushed Conan to the mouth of an alley. "Now will you agree to a plan?"

Malak snatched an orange from a fruit-monger's cart that stood beside the alley. The peddler opened his mouth, looked at the small man's companions, and closed it again.

"Now I see there is no use to a plan," Conan replied slowly. "I must try to rescue her, for I have vowed it, but I fear that I and any who go with me will die in the attempt. It is best the rest of you leave."

"I will go with you," Zula said fiercely. "I owe you a life, and I will follow you until it is repaid."

"You are fools," Akiro said despairingly. "Do

you mean to attack the palace as if you were an army?''

The fruit-monger's mouth fell open.

"What about you, wizard?" Malak asked around a mouthful of orange. "Can you not help with some incantation or spell?"

"No doubt," Akiro said drily, "I could hurl a fireball that would destroy those gates as if they were made of parchment. But I must stand in the open to do it, with the result that someone will probably put a spear in me, leaving the three of you to battle tenscore guards, if not twice so many."

Eyes wide, the fruit-monger threw his weight behind his cart and pushed it away as fast as his legs would carry him.

"That does not sound like such a good idea to me," Malak laughed weakly. "Mitra, who would believe anyone would go to all this trouble to get into that place, considering what my cousin went through to get out."

"I thought your cousin died in those dungeons," Conan said absently. His eyes and his mind were still on the palace and the fast-approaching night.

Malak shook his head, trying to avoid Zula's glaring frown. "Two of them died. One escaped. . . ." He trailed off as Conan swiveled his head to look at him. Akiro raised a quizzical eyebrow. "That is, he did die. All of them died. I know nothing about tunnels or anything of that sort. I don't remember. I swear it!"

"I could break his head," Zula said thoughtfully.

"Then he could not talk," Akiro said. "But he does not need his manhood for speech. I could shrivel that."

Conan merely fingered the hilt of his dagger.

The small thief looked from one pair of eyes to another, then sighed. "Oh, very well. I'll show you."

Conan gestured him to lead on, then followed quickly on his heels as Malak started down the alley.

It was a snaking path the little man took, along alleys slick with offal and stinking of urine and excrement, and it led away from the palace. At last, behind a stone building many streets away, he ducked into a shadowed doorway. The Cimmerian trod on his heels down rough steps in deeper dark and musty air.

"We need light," Conan sighed reluctantly. "Akiro?"

Abruptly there was light, a ball of it resting on the wizard's fingertips. They were in a cellar, filled with sagging crates and splintered barrels. Dust and cobwebs lay thickly on everything. Akiro found a torch among the rubble and transfered the fire from his fingers to that.

"There is a way from this place to a palace?" Zula said disbelievingly.

On hand and knees Malak counted the large, square stones of the floor along one wall. "Here," he said, pointing to one that seemed no different from any other. "This is the one. If I remember it right."

"You had better," Zula said darkly.

Conan knelt by the stone. At one side there was just enough gap for him to get a grip with his fingertips. He pulled the block up, worked his fingers under it, and heaved it over. Below it was a dark hole, slightly smaller than the stone slab. He seized the torch from Akiro and thrust it into the opening. It was walled in stone, and along one side there were holes spaced properly for hands and feet.

"Ah!" said Akiro. "Whoever built that palace was a wise man. However strong a fortress, it is always wisdom to have a bolt-hole or two. I do not doubt there are others."

Conan swung his legs into the hole. "Then it will take us inside the palace walls."

"Are you not forgetting tenscore guards?" Malak demanded. "Sigyn's Bowl, Cimmerian, they will not be one fewer because you are inside."

"You are right," Conan said. "This improves our chances but little. You have done your part, my friend. You need not come further."

Zula spat loudly, and Malak twisted his mouth. "Amphrates' jewels," he breathed heavily, "had best be worth more gold than I think they are."

With a grin Conan began his descent.

XXII

Dusk rolled across Shadizar as Taramis looked down once more upon the courtyard where the Sleeping God lay. The canopy was gone now, and a different circle of golden-robed priests prayed around the god. Her four bodyguards, and six more black-armored warriors hand-picked by Bombatta, stood watch about the courtyard. She did not like that. They knew what they served, but they had never seen any part of the ceremonies, and there should be no outsiders to witness what would happen this night. But Bombatta's stupidity had made it necessary.

True, it was unlikely in the extreme that the thief still lived. Even did he live, surely one man, and he a thief out of the streets, could do nothing to hinder her plans in the slightest. But the Scrolls of Skelos spoke of the possibility . . . no, they spoke of the certainty of danger if the thief lived. And that fool Bombatta had the temerity to sulk somewhere in the palace because she had upbraided him. Something would have to be done about Bombatta when this night was over.

With a last look at the darkening sky, she returned to her chambers. There was much yet to be done.

From the chest of ebony inlaid with silver she took a twist of parchment. Wine she poured from a crystal flagon into a goblet of chased gold. The parchment gave up a white powder which dissolved quickly in the wine. A second goblet stood beside the first on the lacquered tray. It was not sorcery, this potion, but it had no taste and would do its work well, and all spells were forbidden this night save those required by the Rite of Awakening.

She clapped her hands, and, when a slave woman in short white tunic appeared, commanded, "Bid the Lady Jehnna attend me." Soon now, she thought. Soon.

Thrusting the torch ahead of him, Conan ran in a half-crouch down the low-ceilinged tunnel, its stone walls gray with mold.

"Not so fast," Malak complained. "Mitra's Bones, could not whoever built this have given it enough height for a man to stand up?"

"You can almost stand as it is," Zula said,

prodding the small thief to greater speed with her staff in his ribs.

Malak glared at her, but only said, "I hope at least they have stairs at the other end. I don't fancy another climb of fifty paces in the dark."

Conan cursed as the torchlight showed him a blank wall ahead, then he became aware that the ceiling was higher here. He straightened, and found himself in another shaft like the one they had descended, complete with holes along one wall for hands and for feet. Without hesitation he climbed.

"A plan," Akiro called after him hoarsely. "You know not what is up there."

Conan climbed on. It was not easy with the torch in one hand. The method required keeping both feet in place and balancing while the one free hand darted to a higher handhold. A single miss in that quick grab, and the long fall back down the shaft was inevitable. Too, it was a way of climbing that should have been done slowly and carefully, but Conan had no time for being careful. He pushed on as if it were stairsteps he climbed.

At the top of the shaft there was a black iron bracket on one stone wall for the torch, and a foothole on the opposite side of the shaft from those he had climbed, so that a man could straddle it if he did not mind getting close to the torch's flame. The stone above had a ring in its center, no doubt to aid closing the bolt-hole behind refugees should the palace's lords and ladies ever find the need to use the route. There had been none on the stone at the other end, as no one had ever been expected to enter from that direction.

The torch seared Conan's back as he heaved against the stone above him. With a mighty shove he toppled it away from the shaft, and raised his head into a dungeon lit only by the obstructed glow of his torch. The walls were a rough-cut stone, and the floor was covered with pale straw dried to dusty brittleness. A small creature chittered and rustled away as the Cimmerian climbed out.

Pausing only to secure the torch, Conan moved to the thick, iron-bound door. An iron plate on the outside of the door covered a slot for checking on prisoners. A careful push showed the huge lock was not fastened. Slowly he cracked the door, grimacing at the squeal of the crudely-wrought iron hinges. The stone-walled hallway outside was empty and dark.

"You should have waited," Akiro panted, scrambling from the shaft. "You had no way to know what lay on this side of that stone."

"It had to be a dungeon," Conan said. "Malak's cousin could hardly have made his escape from the great hall, or from Taramis' bedchamber."

The old wizard stared at him, astounded. "Logical. I did not expect such thinking from you. You always seem to go at problems with a sword, rather than logical thought."

Malak, who was allowing Zula to help him into the cell, muttered, offended, "How do you know my cousin did not escape from Taramis' bedchamber? All the men of my family have a great attraction for women.''

Zula snorted, and Malak opened his mouth again, but Conan cut short any argument with a sharp gesture. ''Do that later,'' he said, and slipped into the hall.

A choice of direction was easy. One way lay more darkness, the other a glow of light. Dropping his torch on the bare stone floor of the corridor, Conan drew his sword and moved toward the light. Short of the dim glow that spilled into the hall he stopped in consternation.

This was the jailer's chamber, a large cube with a rough cot in one corner, well lit by torches in iron sconces. On the far side stairs led upward, and at a table of crude-hewn planks by those stairs sat the jailer, a big balding man with as much hair on his arms and legs as he had once had on his head. He chewed at a joint of beef held in one thick-fingered hand, while the other scratched casually beneath his leather jerkin. He faced the hall where Conan stood hidden only by darkness, and from where he sat he could be halfway up the stairs shouting an alarm before the Cimmerian could reach the table.

As Conan tensed to take the chance, Zula touched him on the arm and shook her head. Swiftly she doffed the strip of cloth that covered her small breasts. Malak licked his lips ostentatiously, but she ignored him, tucking the cloth into the other piece she wore about her loins. Then, with a welcoming smile on her face, she padded into the jailer's chamber, using her staff as if it were a walking stick.

The balding man froze with the joint half-raised to his mouth. "Where in Zandru's Nine Hells did you come from?" he growled. "You're no prisoner of mine."

Zula did not speak, but the roll of her slim hips increased as she continued toward him.

The jailor tossed the joint onto the table, missing a cracked pottery plate, and scrubbed the back of a broad hand across his greasy mouth as he stood and moved around the table. "If you're not a prisoner, you're not supposed to be here," he said thickly. "And being where you're not supposed to be can get you put to the question. Painful, that. Why don't you talk? You got a tongue? No matter. If you want to avoid the hot irons and the strapado, wench, you're going to treat me like a walking god and the love of your life, all rolled into one."

He reached for her, then. Zula's face did not change as her staff, suddenly gripped with two hands, whipped up into the big man's crotch. A strangled squawk burst from his throat, and his eyes bulged almost out of his fat face. He doubled over, and her staff whirled around to crack the side of his balding head. With a sigh, he crumpled to the floor stones. Calmly Zula donned her halter once more.

"Most effective," Akiro said with a smile, as

the others joined her. Malak studiously avoided looking at her bosom even after she was covered.

Conan did not wait for talk. The coming of
night weighed him like massive stones on his
shoulders. Sword in hand, he raced up the stairs,
barely hearing the clatter as the rest followed behind.

"You sent for me, my aunt?" Jehnna said from
the door.

Taramis put on a smile, pleasant and, she
believed, familial. One more role the girl had to fill,
she thought, and for that Jehnna had been prepared
well. Thin black silk covered her to the floor,
hugging her slender curves. Her black hair, dressed
simply, flowed about her shoulders, and her face
was bare of any trace of kohl or rouge. A scrubbed
face for innocence, and black silk for the Night.
And the girl's black contrasted well with her own
scarlet silk, slashed to show her voluptuous curves
to best advantage before the god.

"Yes, child," Taramis answered. "This is your
natal day, and tonight you fulfill your destiny.
Come, drink a celebration cup with me." She
filled the second goblet, then held out the first to
the girl. "You are a woman, now, and old enough
for wine."

Jehnna took the goblet hesitantly, peering at the
dark ruby liquid within. "I have often wondered
about wine," she said.

"Drink," Taramis told her. "Drink deeply. It is
best so." She held her breath while Jehnna hesi-

tated further, then let it out when the slender girl raised the goblet, drinking as commanded, deeply.

Jehnna gave a little laugh as she lowered the almost empty goblet. "It warms so, swirling all through me it seems."

"Do you feel lightheaded? That happens, sometimes."

"I feel. . . . I feel. . . ." Jehnna trailed off with a slight giggle.

Tarmis took the golden cup from unresisting fingers and studied the girl's large eyes. Wine would not act so fast, even on one so unfamiliar with it as Jehnna, but the powder should. It *had* to have taken effect. "Kneel, child," she said.

Smiling as if it were the most ordinary thing to be told to do, Jehnna knelt.

The powder worked quite as well as a spell, Taramis thought. There would be no hesitation at a fatal moment. Aloud, she said, "Stand up, child." Even as Jehnna rose she went on. "Xanteres! She is ready."

The mild-faced high priest hurried into the room with the golden casket in his hands. He reached to open it himself, but Taramis brushed his thin hand aside. It was her place to do this. When the casket lid was lifted, she barely saw the glowing Heart of Ahriman. On the morrow, when it was safe for her to touch the stone, many wonders of great power could she do with the Heart. Tonight, only the Horn of Dagoth had importance.

"Take up the Horn, child," Taramis said, then

watched jealously as Jehnna's fingers curled around its curving golden length.

In the courtyard four brazen gongs sounded their rolling tones. Full night drew nigh.

"Come, child," Taramis said. And, bearing the Horn of Dagoth before her, Jehnna followed toward her destiny.

Treading carefully, silently, Conan made his way down a palace corridor, unheeding of rare Vendhyan carpets on the marble floor or ancient Iranistani tapestries lining the walls where golden lamps flickered. Warily his companions followed him. Taramis' guards were everywhere. Twice already they had been forced to hide in a crossing hall, Conan gritting his teeth in frustration, while half a score of the black-armored men marched past. As much as urgency spurred him, it would be impossible to engage such a squad without an alarm being given. And Jehnna *must* be found before any alarm, if there was to be a hope of getting her out alive.

The Cimmerian stepped into the intersection of two corridors, and the creak of leather gave him a chance to live. On either side of him, leaning against the wall where he could not see them before, was a guard in ebon breastplate and nasaled helm. Their hands streaked for their swords as he appeared. There was no time to think of what to do; he must act.

With a two-handed grip on his hilt Conan pivoted to the left, driving his blade through the guard's breastplate while the other's sword was yet half-drawn. In one motion he pulled his steel free and continued his spin. The other man had his tulwar drawn, and was making the mistake of raising it to slash rather than thrusting. The tip of Conan's streaking blade slashed across the undersides of the man's upraised arms. As the guard jerked his arms down in reflex at the agony, Conan completed his turn, taking a step closer as his sword twisted in a narrow loop and bit deeply into the black helmet. The second corpse struck the marble floor within a heartbeat of the first.

Malak whistled in admiration, and Zula stared in awe. "You are fast," she breathed. "Never have I seen—"

"These men," Conan cut her off, "will be found soon, or missed, whether we hide them or not."

"You mean the ten score guards are going to know we're here?" Malak's voice was shrill. "Danh's Bony Rump!"

"Go back to the dungeon," Zula said scornfully. "The way out is yet open."

Malak grimaced, then drew his daggers. "I always wanted to be a hero," he said weakly.

Conan growled them all to silence. "I mean there is no more time for caution. We must find Jehnna. *Quickly.*" Like a hunting leopard he sped on, driven by the darkness that thickened the sky outside.

*   *   *

A gasp of awe rose from the assembled priests—
all of them were there, now—when the small procession entered the courtyard, and Taramis basked
in it. She knew it was for the girl behind her, for
the One and the golden Horn of Dagoth that she
bore, but she, Taramis, had brought it to be.

The voluptuous noblewoman stepped aside, revealing Jehnna and her burden clearly, and the
golden-robed priests fell to their knees. Xanteres,
who had exchanged the casket for his tall staff of
gold tipped with its azure diamond eye, moved to
the other side of the girl, stroking his full white
beard in self-satisfaction, to gain his share of the
adulation.

"The Sleeping God will never die," Taramis
intoned.

"Where there is faith," came the response from
the kneeling priests, "there is no death."

She flung wide her arms. "This is the Night of
Awakening," she cried, "for the One has come!"
The reply echoed from the walls.

"All glory to the One, who serves the Sleeping
God!"

The half score black-armored guards, their spears
precisely slanted, but standing well back so as to
be out of the way, shifted uneasily. From the
colonnade came the piping of flutes, beginning
their litany of coming sacrifice and anointment.
The velvet black sky arched above, glittering stars

set in a pattern they would not attain again for another thousand years. The moment had come.

Power, Taramis thought while the echos still shivered the air. Power and immortality were hers.

Conan slid to a halt as a man stepped into the corridor ahead of him, a man black-armored and even more massive than he, with a naked tulwar in his hand.

"I knew you must come this way, thief," Bombatta said softly. His scarred face was grimmer than ever before behind the nasal of his sable helm. "When I found the bodies, I knew then that you lived. And I knew you would run to the great court to save her. But if I cannot have Jehnna, no mortal man will have her." His blade came up, gleaming in the lamplight. "She goes to the god, thief."

Motioning the others to hang back, Conan moved closer. In the confines of the tapestried hall they could only hinder, not help. The Cimmerian gripped his sword with both hands, holding it erect before him.

"Have you lost your tongue?" Bombatta demanded. "In moments the girl dies in the very center of this palace, I tell you. Rage at your loss, thief. Let me know your despair and lose my own in the slaying of you."

"This is no time for talking," Conan replied. "It is a time for dying."

The two blades moved, then, as one. The clang-

ing of steel on steel filled the hall as they wove a
deadly lace between the two big men. Attack and
counterattack, thrust and riposte, followed so closely
one on the other that it seemed as though lightning
flashed and danced.

Abruptly Conan's broadsword was torn from his
grasp. Triumph flared in Bombatta's face, but even
as the blow struck Conan's foot lashed out, sending the giant Zamoran's blade spinning. The two
men crashed together, grappling. For an instant
each strove to reach his dagger, then Bombatta's
huge hands closed on Conan's head and twisted,
and the Cimmerian gripped the black helm, one
hand on its bottom edge, the other above the dark
nasal. Feet shifted and scuffled for balance, and
hard-drawn breath was the sound of battle, now.
Massive thews bulged, and joints popped with the
strain.

A grinding crack sounded, not loud, yet seeming to drown all else, and Conan found that he
supported a boneless mass. For an instant he stared
into those black eyes, as death filmed them, then
let Bombatta fall.

"Time is running out," Zula said, "and we still
do not know where to find her."

Working his neck, Conan retrieved his sword.
"But we do. He told us. The great court in the
center of the palace."

"He also said she was to die in moments,"
Malak reminded him.

"Then there is no time to stand here talking,"
Conan said. "Come."

* * *

"O great Dagoth," Taramis intoned, "on the Night of Awakening we, thy servants, come to thee."

The flutes shrilled madly as she took Jehnna's arm. Xanteres took the other, and between them they led the girl to the head of the great reclining form of the god, its noble forehead marred by the dark, circular depression. Holding the Horn before her, Jehnna moved unresistingly.

"O great Dagoth," the tall princess chanted, "on the Night of Awakening, thy servants call to thee." In a whisper she spoke to Jehnna. "The Horn, child. Place the Horn as you were told."

Jehnna blinked, hesitated, and Taramis' breath caught at the fear that the potion's effect might have worn off. Then slowly the slender girl set the base of the golden Horn into the depression in Dagoth's forehead.

A tremor passed through the huge, alabastrine form. Marble hardness softened, and took on the hue of human skin. The eyelids fluttered.

Relief flooded through Taramis. Nothing could halt it, now. The Sleeping God was awaking. And the Horn was no longer sacrosanct to Dagoth and the One, alone. But it all had to be finished, and quickly now.

"O great Dagoth," she called, "accept this, our offering and pledge to thee. Accept thy third anointing, the Anointing of the One."

Jehnna did not even start as Xanteres tangled his

left hand in her hair and bent her forward over the recumbent god's head. A gilded dagger flashed in his hand as he raised it.

Bursting into the great courtyard, Conan took in the scene before him, the black-armored guards, the kneeling priests in gold, the huge, horned form that seemed to be just beginning to stir. And Jehnna, throat arched for the knife in the hands of the white-bearded man.

An instant it took him to see, and in that same instant he was moving. His sword was tossed from right hand to left, the fisted pommel smashed into the ebon helmet of a guard, his right hand tore the spear from the guard's grasp. As the dagger moved toward Jehnna he threw. The spear lanced a dark streak across the courtyard, and the dagger dropped to the marble tiles as the white-bearded man, a wavering shriek rising from his throat, clutched at the thick black shaft that pierced him.

An instant, and in that instant the courtyard swirled into chaos. Black-armored guards turned to battle Conan, who suddenly found Malak fighting at his side. Zula dashed across the court, beating golden-robed priests from her path with her staff, to seize Jehnna's arm and drag her away from the huge, now-quivering form.

"There is yet time," Taramis screamed. "It must be done! It must be!" On hand and knees she scrambled for the fallen dagger.

And the huge form of Dagoth sat up, the shape

of a gigantic man, too handsome for humankind, with a golden horn standing out from his forehead. The air in the court turned chill as it moved, and no man or woman there but froze. The noble head turned, great golden eyes surveying the courtyard. Then suddenly the head was thrown back, and Dagoth howled. Staggering to his feet, he howled such agony as had never been known on the face of the earth.

As if the terrible sound had freed him from paralysis, Conan found he could move again. He gripped his sword and set himself, but the guards before him threw down their spears and fled, brushing past him as if what else was in that courtyard made the steel in his hands no longer worth fearing.

Dagoth's form rippled, now, as though knots grew beneath the skin. Bulging, writhing, it grew and changed. In the twinkling of an eye its skin became coarse. The brow sloped back, and the jaw grew forward, fangs thrusting past lips. Arms and legs thickened, and claws sprouted on the ends of fingers. The skin of the back split, and leathery wings as of a monstrous bat came forth. Grotesquely male, hunched and twisted, yet three times the height of a man, Dagoth stood, and only the huge golden eyes were unchanged.

Those eyes came to rest on Taramis, kneeling with the dagger clutched to her breasts and her face slack with horror. "You!" It was as if thunder had spoken, and with the tongue of thunder.

"Out of your own mouth, Taramis, are you promised to me!"

Hope dawned on Taramis's face. "Yes," she breathed. Leaping to her feet she ran toward the god. "I am promised to thee," she cried. "And thou wilt gift me with power and immortality. Thou wilt—"

Clawed hands pulled the noblewoman to Dagoth, and the huge wings folded around them, hiding her. From beneath those wings came a crystalline wail of purest pain and disbelief. The wings opened, and Dagoth tossed aside a robe of scarlet silk.

"Thus it is," the thunder roared, "to know a god, and be known by a god!"

Zula had stopped to stare in horror at the garment that was all that remained of Taramis, and Jehnna stood beside her, seemingly unaware of what occurred about her.

Dashing forward, Conan grabbed each woman in turn, pushing them toward the shelter of the palace. "Run!" he commanded, and they ran.

"No, mortal!" Came the thunder. "She is the One, and the One is mine!"

Conan felt the ground tremble as Dagoth took a step. The women could never outdistance that monstrous form. Time would have to be bought for them. Certain for the first time in his life that he faced something he could not defeat, Conan turned to confront the god.

Suddenly a fireball streaked over his head to strike Dagoth's chest. It bounced away like a pebble from a mountain, yet even as it did another struck, and another. "Run, Cimmerian!" Akiro shouted. "Erlik take you, run! I cannot hold such as this forever!"

Dagoth's wings stiffened, then snapped together behind his back like a thunderclap. And as if that sound had called invisible lightning Akiro was flung into the air and hurled backwards.

"And you, mortal!" Dagoth thundered at Conan. "Would you oppose a god? Know the fear of what you do."

Then did Conan feel fear rolling over him, fear primordial, fear so strong that it felt as though his very bones would split asunder. Overpowering waves of it crashed on him, pushing that which called itself Conan of Cimmeria back, back beyond knowledge of civilization or fire or speech, back to the ancient creature that knew no gods, the creature that survived its lack of claws and fangs because it was more deadly than leopard or bear. That creature knew but one response to fear. With a roar the cave sloth knew and feared, Conan attacked.

His broadsword slashed deep, and Dagoth laughed like a storm at sea as bloodless wounds healed even as they were made. Claw-tipped hands seized the Cimmerian, lifted him toward gaping fangs, and still Conan hacked with a mad fury that would not quit till death overtook him.

Yet as he fought, dim words penetrated Conan's brain. "The horn!" Part of him struggled to listen, while the greater part raged to kill. Akiro, that small part thought. "He is only vulnerable through the horn!" the wizard shouted.

Conan was raised before the golden eyes, and he returned their gaze unafraid. Fear had been purged from him by the blood-red madness that screamed to slay or die.

The Cimmerian laughed as he let his sword fall and seized the horn; it was like seizing lightning, yet he voiced his deathly grim laughter. Massive shoulders knotted, he tore the golden horn from that monstrous head. Pain flared in the god's xanthic eyes, and the fanged mouth opened wider to rip at the human who had wounded him. But the insane rage of the attacker had not left Conan. As he ripped the horn free, he reversed it, thrust it point first into one of the golden globes that stared at him, shoved it deep with all his might.

The howl that Dagoth had loosed before was a whisper to the scream that came from him now. Conan was flung through the air, spinning end over end, to crash to the marble tiles. Higher and higher the shriek rose. Suddenly it could not be heard at all, but now the Cimmerian's skull vibrated, and white-hot daggers bored at his ears. Clawing at his head, he struggled to rise. He must fight. He must kill. He must. . . .

A measure of sanity returned to him amid the pain as he realized that he was seeing stars. *Through* Dagoth. The gigantic shape still loomed in the center of the courtyard, clawed hands clutching its face, blood like rubies welling between the taloned fingers, the blood of a god dropping to shatter like crystal on the marble beneath his feet, but even as the Cimmerian watched the form grew dimmer, less distinct. In gossamer outline Dagoth hung against the night sky. Abruptly he was gone, and with him the pain from Conan's head.

Unsteadily the Cimmerian surveyed the courtyard. The priests were fled, and of the black-armored guards none remained save those he and Malak had slain. Zula crouched beside Jehnna, cradling the slender girl in her arms. "She collapsed," the black woman told Conan, "when you tore out that horn. But it is only a sleep, I think. She will be well."

"Hey, Conan," Malak called. The small thief was propped against the marble pillar of the colonnade. Akiro, who moved as if he were one bruise from head to foot, was binding a cloth about Malak's bloody thigh. "I took a spear, but we won. Hannuman's Stones, man, we won!"

"Perhaps," Conan said tiredly. He grasped the dragon amulet on his chest as if he would crush it. "Perhaps."

epilogue

From an alabaster balcony of the vast marble palace that had once been Taramis', Conan watched the sun rise from the far horizon. It was the second time he had watched a sunrise from that same spot. A day and a night to rest and think, to reach decisions. He had made his decisions, then given a few commands, and showed a handbreadth of steel when those commands were questioned.

"My Lord Conan," said a servant behind him, "the Princess Jehnna b-begs your presence." The woman blushed, flustered at stammering, flustered because a Zamoran noblewoman never begged. Most especially not a princess.

"I am not a lord," Conan said, then quickly added, "Take me to the Princess Jehnna," before she could become flustered further.

The tapestry-hung chamber to which he was led was meant for informal audiences, with a dais only one step high and an unadorned, high-backed chair of polished ebony for a throne. Jehnna looked well on it, he thought, in her robes of white silk. The others were much recovered from their ordeals as well, Malak surreptitiously fingering a golden bowl, Akiro looking impatient with a bundle of tightly rolled scrolls under his arm, Zula leaning on her staff near Jehnna's throne as if she were a body-guard.

"Conan," Jehnna said brightly as he entered, "it has come. King Tiridates has invested me as Princess Royal of Zamora and confirmed me in Taramis' estates."

"I congratulate you," he said, and she frowned at him doubtfully.

The frown cleared quickly though, and she said, "I have asked you all to come to me this morning because I have a favor to ask of each of you. You, first, Malak." The small man jerked his hand from the bowl as if burned. "I ask you to remain here with me, Malak," she went on, "living in my palace. Thus I will always be reminded that a man can be a fool, yet be brave and good."

"Even my mother never called me good," Malak said slowly. His eyes drifted to the bowl. "But I will stay in your palace. For a time."

"Best to put a guard on him, then," Akiro said drily, and grinned at the offended glare he got from Malak.

"You, also, Akiro," Jehnna said, "must stay with me. You are a man of great wisdom, and I will need wise counsel in the days, the years, to come."

"Impossible," the wizard replied. "You have given me the Scrolls of Skelos, and some bush-shamans on the Kothian border are carrying on vile practices that I have vowed to end."

"I can put soldiers at your disposal to deal with the shamans," Jehnna told him, then added slyly, "And Taramis gathered several rooms full of magical volumes and instruments which you would be free to study for as long as you remained here."

"Soldiers," Akiro mused. "I suppose soldiers could deal with such hedge-shamans as those. Ah, how many rooms full, exactly?"

"Many," Jehnna laughed. "Zula, you must stay, as well. You have showed me that a woman need not be confined by others' boundaries, but there is much yet to teach. The staff, for instance."

The black woman sighed regretfully. "I cannot. I owe a life to Conan, and I must follow him until I can re—"

"No!" Conan said sharply. "The debt cannot be repaid in that way."

"But—"

"It cannot, Zula. It has come to me that some debts cannot be repaid directly the one owed. Find another life to save, and I will be repaid by that."

Zula nodded slowly before turning back to Jehnna. "I will stay, Jehnna, and gladly."

"Conan," Jehnna said, and hurried on when he opened his mouth. "Listen to me, Conan. Stay with me. Sit beside me."

"I cannot," Conan said gently.

"But why not? By all the gods, I want you, and I need you."

"I live by my wits and my sword. Would you have me become a lapdog? 'Tis all I could be, here. I am not made for palaces and silks."

"Then I will go with you," she said, and stiffened when he laughed.

"The Turanians have a saying, Jehnna. The eagle does not run in the hills, the leopard does not fly in the sky. You would take to my life as ill as I would take to yours. Never a day but I must fight for my life or ride for it. That is the road I travel, and you cannot come with me."

"But, Conan—"

"Fare you well, Jehnna, and all the gods grant you happiness."

He turned his back on her then, and walked from the room. He thought he heard her call after him, but he would not look back or listen. As he had commanded, his horse waited, saddled, before the palace.

The sun was almost to its zenith by the time he reached the rough stone altar on the plains. The wind had swept dirt and sand against it, and he thought Malak might have some difficulty finding exactly where Amphrates' jewels were buried, but otherwise nothing had changed.

Slipping the dragon amulet from about his neck, he laid it on the altar. From his pouch he took the vial Akiro had given him. So long ago, it seemed. Some debts could not be repaid to the one to whom they were owed.

"Fare you well, Valeria," he said softly. And, scraping the seal from the vial, he drank.

Heat rushed along his limbs, and he squeezed his eyes shut, his horse dancing from an involuntary jerk on the reins. When he opened them again, the heat was gone. He found shards of a vial crushed in his fist, and wondered how they had come there. A glint of gold in the sun caught his eye. A pendant, he saw, in the shape of a dragon, resting atop a strange pile of stones. He bent from the saddle, but before his fingers touched the gold, he stopped. There was something, something he did not understand, that told him he should not take it. Sorcery, he decided.

Well, there was gold aplenty in Shadizar that was not sorcerous, and willing wenches to sit on his knee and help spend all he stole. With a laugh, he kicked his horse into a gallop for the city. Never once was he tempted to look back.

THE DRAGON REBORN

sequel to *The Great Hunt*

Book Three
of
The Wheel of Time

by

Robert Jordan

Praise for *Eye of the World*

"A powerful vision of good and evil...fascinating people moving through a rich and interesting world." —*Orson Scott Card*

"Richly detailed...fully realized, complex adventure."
—*Library Journal*

"A combination of Robin Hood and Stephen King that is hard to resist...Jordan makes the reader care about these characters as though they were old friends." —*Milwaukee Sentinel*

Praise for *The Great Hunt*

"Jordan can spin as rich a world and as event-filled a tale as [Tolkien]...will not be easy to put down." —*ALA Booklist*

"Worth re-reading a time or two." —*Locus*

"This is good stuff...Splendidly characterized and cleverly plotted...The Great Hunt is a good book which will always be a good book. I shall certainly [line up] for the third volume."
—*Interzone*

The Dragon Reborn
coming in hardcover in August, 1991

Robert Jordan's
THE EYE OF THE WORLD

The acclaimed first volume of
The Wheel of Time

"This one is as solid as a steel blade, and glowing
with the true magic. Robert Jordan deserves
congratulations."   —Fred Saberhagen

"The next major fantasy epic!"   —Piers Anthony

"A splendid epic of heroic fantasy, vast in scope,
colorful in detail, and convincing in its presentation
of human character and personality."

—L. Sprague de Camp

☐
☐ 51181-6

$5.95
Canada $6.95

THE MIGHTY ADVENTURES OF CONAN

☐☐	55210-5	CONAN THE BOLD *John Maddox Roberts*	$3.95 Canada $4.95
☐☐	50094-6	CONAN THE CHAMPION *John Maddox Roberts*	$3.95 Canada $4.95
☐☐	51394-0	CONAN THE DEFENDER *Robert Jordan*	$3.95 Canada $4.95
☐☐	54264-9	CONAN THE DEFIANT *Steve Perry*	$6.95 Canada $8.95
☐☐	50096-2	CONAN THE FEARLESS *Steve Perry*	$3.95 Canada $4.95
☐☐	50998-6	CONAN THE FORMIDABLE *Steve Perry*	$7.95 Canada $9.50
☐☐	50690-1	CONAN THE FREE LANCE *Steve Perry*	$3.95 Canada $4.95
☐☐	50714-2	CONAN THE GREAT *Leonard Carpenter*	$3.95 Canada $4.95
☐☐	50961-7	CONAN THE GUARDIAN *Roland Green*	$3.95 Canada $4.95
☐☐	50860-2	CONAN THE INDOMITABLE *Steve Perry*	$3.95 Canada $4.95
☐☐	50997-8	CONAN THE INVINCIBLE *Robert Jordan*	$3.95 Canada $4.95

Buy them at your local bookstore or use this handy coupon:
Clip and mail this page with your order.

Publishers Book and Audio Mailing Service
P.O. Box 120159, Staten Island, NY 10312-0004

Please send me the book(s) I have checked above. I am enclosing $ _____
(please add $1.25 for the first book, and $.25 for each additional book to cover postage and handling.
Send check or money order only—no CODs).

Name _____

Address _____

City _____ State/Zip _____

Please allow six weeks for delivery. Prices subject to change without notice.

FANTASY BESTSELLERS
FROM TOR

☐	55852-9	ARIOSTO	$3.95
☐	55853-7	*Chelsea Quinn Yarbro*	Canada $4.95
☐	53671-1	THE DOOR INTO FIRE	$2.95
☐	53672-X	*Diane Duane*	Canada $3.50
☐	53673-8	THE DOOR INTO SHADOW	$2.95
☐	53674-6	*Diane Duane*	Canada $3.50
☐	55750-6	ECHOES OF VALOR	$2.95
☐	55751-4	*edited by Karl Edward Wagner*	Canada $3.95
☐	51181-6	THE EYE OF THE WORLD	$5.95
☐		*Robert Jordan*	Canada $6.95
☐	53388-7	THE HIDDEN TEMPLE	$3.95
☐	53389-5	*Catherine Cooke*	Canada $4.95
☐	55446-9	MOONSINGER'S FRIENDS	$3.50
☐	55447-7	*edited by Susan Shwartz*	Canada $4.50
☐	55515-5	THE SHATTERED HORSE	$3.95
☐	55516-3	*S.P. Somtow*	Canada $4.95
☐	50249-3	SISTER LIGHT, SISTER DARK	$3.95
☐	50250-7	*Jane Yolen*	Canada $4.95
☐	54348-3	SWORDSPOINT	$3.95
☐	54349-1	*Ellen Kushner*	Canada $4.95
☐	53293-7	THE VAMPIRE TAPESTRY	$2.95
☐	53294-5	*Suzie McKee Charnas*	Canada $3.95

Buy them at your local bookstore or use this handy coupon:
Clip and mail this page with your order.

Publishers Book and Audio Mailing Service
P.O. Box 120159, Staten Island, NY 10312-0004

Please send me the book(s) I have checked above. I am enclosing $ _____
(Please add $1.25 for the first book, and $.25 for each additional book to cover postage and handling.
Send check or money order only—no CODs.)

Name _____

Address _____

City _____ State/Zip _____

Please allow six weeks for delivery. Prices subject to change without notice.

MORE BESTSELLING
FANTASY FROM TOR

☐ ☐	50556-5	THE BEWITCHMENTS OF LOVE AND HATE *Storm Constantine*	$4.95 Canada $5.95
☐ ☐	50554-9	THE ENCHANTMENTS OF FLESH AND SPIRIT *Storm Constantine*	$3.95 Canada $4.95
☐ ☐	54600-8	THE FLAME KEY *Robert E. Vardeman*	$2.95 Canada $3.95
☐ ☐	54606-7	KEY OF ICE AND STEEL *Robert E. Vardeman*	$3.50 Canada $4.50
☐ ☐	53239-2	SCHIMMELHORN'S GOLD *Reginald Bretnor*	$ 2.95 Canada $ 3.75
☐ ☐	54602-4	THE SKELETON LORD'S KEY *Robert E. Vardeman*	$2.95 Canada $3.95
☐ ☐	55825-1	SNOW WHITE AND ROSE RED *Patricia C. Wrede*	$3.95 Canada $4.95
☐ ☐	55350-0	THE SWORDSWOMAN *Jessica Amanda Salmonson*	$3.50 Canada $4.50
☐ ☐	54402-1	THE UNICORN DILEMMA *John Lee*	$3.95 Canada $4.95
☐ ☐	54400-5	THE UNICORN QUEST *John Lee*	$2.95 Canada $3.50
☐ ☐	50907-2	WHITE JENNA *Jane Yolen*	$3.95 Canada $4.95

Buy them at your local bookstore or use this handy coupon:
Clip and mail this page with your order.

Publishers Book and Audio Mailing Service
P.O. Box 120159, Staten Island, NY 10312-0004

Please send me the book(s) I have checked above. I am enclosing $ _____
(please add $1.25 for the first book, and $.25 for each additional book to cover postage and handling.
Send check or money order only—no CODs).

Name _____
Address _____
City _____ State/Zip _____
Please allow six weeks for delivery. Prices subject to change without notice.

THE BEST IN
SCIENCE FICTION

☐	54310-6	A FOR ANYTHING	$3.95
☐	54311-4	*Damon Knight*	Canada $4.95
☐	55625-9	BRIGHTNESS FALLS FROM THE AIR	$3.50
☐	55626-7	*James Tiptree, Jr.*	Canada $3.95
☐	53815-3	CASTING FORTUNE	$3.95
☐	53816-1	*John M. Ford*	Canada $4.95
☐	50554-9	THE ENCHANTMENTS OF FLESH & SPIRIT	$3.95
☐	50555-7	*Storm Constantine*	Canada $4.95
☐	55413-2	HERITAGE OF FLIGHT	$3.95
☐	55414-0	*Susan Shwartz*	Canada $4.95
☐	54293-2	LOOK INTO THE SUN	$3.95
☐	54294-0	*James Patrick Kelly*	Canada $4.95
☐	54925-2	MIDAS WORLD	$2.95
☐	54926-0	*Frederik Pohl*	Canada $3.50
☐	53157-4	THE SECRET ASCENSION	$4.50
☐	53158-2	*Michael Bishop*	Canada $5.50
☐	55627-5	THE STARRY RIFT	$4.50
☐	55628-3	*James Tiptree, Jr.*	Canada $5.50
☐	50623-5	TERRAPLANE	$3.95
☐		*Jack Womack*	Canada $4.95
☐	50369-4	WHEEL OF THE WINDS	$3.95
☐	50370-8	*M.J. Engh*	Canada $4.95

Buy them at your local bookstore or use this handy coupon:
Clip and mail this page with your order.

Publishers Book and Audio Mailing Service
P.O. Box 120159, Staten Island, NY 10312-0004

Please send me the book(s) I have checked above. I am enclosing $ _____
(Please add $1.25 for the first book, and $.25 for each additional book to cover postage and handling.
Send check or money order only—no CODs.)

Name _____
Address _____
City _____ State/Zip _____
Please allow six weeks for delivery. Prices subject to change without notice.

SCIENCE FICTION FROM
PIERS ANTHONY

☐ ☐	53114-0	ANTHONOLOGY	$3.50 Canada $3.95
☐ ☐	53098-5	BUT WHAT OF EARTH?	$4.95 Canada $5.95
☐ ☐	53125-6	DRAGON'S GOLD *with Robert E. Margroff*	$3.95 Canada $4.95
☐ ☐	53105-1	THE E.S.P. WORM	$2.95 Canada $3.95
☐ ☐	53127-2	GHOST	$3.95 Canada $4.95
☐ ☐	53108-6	PRETENDER *with Frances Hall*	$3.50 Canada $3.95
☐ ☐	53116-7	PROSTHO PLUS	$2.95 Canada $3.75
☐ ☐	53101-9	RACE AGAINST TIME	$3.50 Canada $4.50
☐ ☐	50104-7	THE RING *with Robert E. Margroff*	$3.95 Canada $4.95
☐ ☐	50257-4	SERPENT'S SILVER *with Robert E. Margroff*	$4.95 Canada $5.95
☐ ☐	53103-5	SHADE OF THE TREE	$3.95 Canada $4.95

Buy them at your local bookstore or use this handy coupon:
Clip and mail this page with your order.

Publishers Book and Audio Mailing Service
P.O. Box 120159, Staten Island, NY 10312-0004

Please send me the book(s) I have checked above. I am enclosing $ _____
(please add $1.25 for the first book, and $.25 for each additional book to cover postage and handling.
Send check or money order only—no CODs).

Name _____
Address _____
City _____ State/Zip _____
Please allow six weeks for delivery. Prices subject to change without notice.

FANTASY ADVENTURE
FROM GLEN COOK

☐ ☐	50389-9	THE BLACK COMPANY	$3.95 Canada $4.95
☐ ☐	50210-8	DREAMS OF STEEL	$3.95 Canada $4.95
☐ ☐	53379-8	AN ILL FATE MARSHALLING	$3.50 Canada $4.50
☐ ☐	53376-3	REAP THE EAST WIND	$2.95 Canada $3.95
☐ ☐	53382-8	SHADOW GAMES	$3.95 Canada $4.95
☐ ☐	50842-4	SHADOWS LINGER	$3.95 Canada $4.95
☐ ☐	50220-5	THE SILVER SPIKE	$3.95 Canada $4.95
☐ ☐	50307-4	THE SWORDBEARER	$3.95 Canada $4.95
☐ ☐	50929-3	THE TOWER OF FEAR	$3.95 Canada $4.95
☐ ☐	50844-0	THE WHITE ROSE	$3.95 Canada $4.95

Buy them at your local bookstore or use this handy coupon:
Clip and mail this page with your order.

Publishers Book and Audio Mailing Service
P.O. Box 120159, Staten Island, NY 10312-0004

Please send me the book(s) I have checked above. I am enclosing $ _____
(please add $1.25 for the first book, and $.25 for each additional book to cover postage and handling.
Send check or money order only—no CODs).

Name _____
Address _____
City _____ State/Zip _____
Please allow six weeks for delivery. Prices subject to change without notice.

SCIENCE FICTION FROM GORDON R. DICKSON

☐ ☐	53577-4	ALIEN ART	$2.95 Canada $3.95
☐ ☐	53546-4	ARCTURUS LANDING	$3.50 Canada $4.50
☐ ☐	53550-2	BEYOND THE DAR AL-HARB	$2.95 Canada $3.50
☐ ☐	53544-8	THE FAR CALL	$4.95 Canada $5.95
☐ ☐	53589-8	GUIDED TOUR	$3.50 Canada $4.50
☐ ☐	53068-3	HOKA! with Poul Anderson	$2.95 Canada $3.50
☐ ☐	53592-8	HOME FROM THE SHORE	$3.50 Canada $4.50
☐ ☐	53562-6	THE LAST MASTER	$2.95 Canada $3.50
☐ ☐	53554-5	LOVE NOT HUMAN	$2.95 Canada $3.95
☐ ☐	53581-2	THE MAN FROM EARTH	$2.95 Canada $3.95
☐ ☐	53572-3	THE MAN THE WORLDS REJECTED	$2.95 Canada $3.75

Buy them at your local bookstore or use this handy coupon:
Clip and mail this page with your order.

Publishers Book and Audio Mailing Service
P.O. Box 120159, Staten Island, NY 10312-0004

Please send me the book(s) I have checked above. I am enclosing $ _____
(please add $1.25 for the first book, and $.25 for each additional book to cover postage and handling.
Send check or money order only—no CODs).

Name _____

Address _____

City _____ State/Zip _____

Please allow six weeks for delivery. Prices subject to change without notice.

SCIENCE FICTION FROM
L.E. MODESITT, JR.

54582-6	THE ECOLITAN OPERATION	$3.95
54583-4		Canada $4.95
54584-2	THE ECOLOGIC ENVOY	$2.95
54585-0		Canada $3.75
50348-1	THE ECOLOGIC SECESSION	$3.95
		Canada $4.95

ANDRE NORTON
THE GRANDE DAME OF SF

FANTASY ADVENTURE
FROM FRED SABERHAGEN

☐	55343-8	THE FIRST BOOK OF SWORDS	$3.95
☐	55344-6		Canada $4.95
☐	55340-3	THE SECOND BOOK OF SWORDS	$3.95
☐	55339-X		Canada $4.95
☐	55345-4	THE THIRD BOOK OF SWORDS	$3.95
☐	55346-2		Canada $4.95
☐	55337-3	THE FIRST BOOK OF LOST SWORDS	$3.95
☐	55338-1		Canada $4.95
☐	55296-2	THE SECOND BOOK OF LOST SWORDS	$3.95
☐	55297-0		Canada $4.95
☐	55288-1	THE THIRD BOOK OF LOST SWORDS	$4.50
☐	55289-X		Canada $5.50
☐	55284-9	THE FOURTH BOOK OF LOST SWORDS	$4.50
☐	55285-7		Canada $5.50
☐	55286-5	THE FIFTH BOOK OF LOST SWORDS	$4.50
☐			Canada $5.50
☐	51118-2	THE SIXTH BOOK OF LOST SWORDS	$4.50
☐			Canada $5.50
☐	50855-6	DOMINION	$3.95
☐			Canada $4.95
☐	50255-8	THE HOLMES-DRACULA FILE	$3.95
☐	50256-6		Canada $4.95
☐	50316-3	THORN	$4.95
☐	50317-1		Canada $5.95

Buy them at your local bookstore or use this handy coupon:
Clip and mail this page with your order.

Publishers Book and Audio Mailing Service
P.O. Box 120159, Staten Island, NY 10312-0004

Please send me the book(s) I have checked above. I am enclosing $ _____
(Please add $1.25 for the first book, and $.25 for each additional book to cover postage and handling.
Send check or money order only—no CODs.)

Name _____

Address _____

City _____ State/Zip _____

Please allow six weeks for delivery. Prices subject to change without notice.

TOR SCIENCE FICTION
DOUBLES

☐	50010-5	THE BLIND GEOMETER	Robinson	$3.50
☐	50114-4	THE NEW ATLANTIS	LeGuin	Canada $4.50
☐	55952-5	BORN WITH THE DEAD	Silverberg	$2.95
☐	55953-3	THE SALIVA TREE	Aldiss	Canada $3.95
☐	55964-9	THE COLOR OF NEANDERTHAL EYES	Tiptree	$3.50
☐	50204-3	AND STRANGE AT ECBATAN THE TREES	Bishop	Canada $4.50
☐	50362-7	DIVIDE AND RULE	de Camp	$3.50
☐	50363-5	THE SWORD OF RHIANNON	Brackett	Canada $4.50
☐	50275-2	ELEGY FOR ANGELS AND DOGS	Williams	$3.50
☐		THE GRAVEYARD HEART	Zelazny	Canada $4.50
☐	55963-0	ENEMY MINE	Longyear	$2.95
☐	54302-5	ANOTHER ORPHAN	Kessel	Canada $3.95
☐	50854-8	EYE FOR EYE	Card	$3.95
☐		THE TUNESMITH	Biggle	Canada $4.95
☐	50813-0	FUGUE STATE	Ford	$3.50
☐		THE DEATH OF DOCTOR ISLAND	Wolfe	Canada $4.50
☐	55971-1	HARDFOUGHT	Bear	$3.50
☐	55951-7	CASCADE POINT	Zahn	Canada $4.50
☐	55879-0	HE WHO SHAPES	Zelazny	$2.95
☐	50266-3	THE INFINITY BOX	Wilhelm	Canada $3.95
☐	50983-8	HOME IS THE HANGMAN	Zelazny	$3.50
☐		WE, IN SOME STRANGE POWER'S EMPLOY,		Canada $4.50
		MOVE ON A RIGOROUS LINE	Delany	

Buy them at your local bookstore or use this handy coupon:
Clip and mail this page with your order.

Publishers Book and Audio Mailing Service
P.O. Box 120159, Staten Island, NY 10312-0004

Please send me the book(s) I have checked above. I am enclosing $ _____
(Please add $1.25 for the first book, and $.25 for each additional book to cover postage and handling.
Send check or money order only—no CODs.)

Name _____
Address _____
City _____ State/Zip _____
Please allow six weeks for delivery. Prices subject to change without notice.